Eric Delderfield's Book of
TRUE ANIMAL STORIES

CONDITIONS OF SALE

Eric Delderfield's Book of

TRUE ANIMAL STORIES

A Piccolo Book

PAN BOOKS LTD : LONDON

First published 1970 by David & Charles (Publishers)
Ltd.
This edition published 1972 by Pan Books Ltd,
33 Tothill Street, London, S.W.1.

ISBN 0 330 02832 4

Printed in Great Britain by
Cox & Wyman Ltd., London, Reading and Fakenham

Contents

List of Illustrations   vii

Introduction   ix

Man's Debt to the Animal World   1

The Things They Do   9

The World of the Horse   49

Rescuers and Rescued   69

Animal Friendships   93

The Battersea Dogs' Home   107

When a Dread Disease Arrived   115

Notable Wild Ones   119

Epilogue   129

ILLUSTRATIONS IN PHOTOGRAVURE

between pages 54 and 55

Amused, apprehensive, curious kittens

Watch your step, brother

Youth at the donkey farm

Bill the badger
(*By courtesy of Mrs A. S. Gaskell*)

Ralph the Alsatian
(*By courtesy of Tony Dibnah*)

Bounce the roe deer
(*By courtesy of Donald MacCastill*)

Pageantry and patience

Police horses being schooled

between pages 70 and 71

A stray at the Battersea Dogs' Home

Dray horses wild with delight
(*By courtesy of Whitbread and Co Ltd*)

Boots and Tiger

Shuna shares her meal
(*By courtesy of Donald MacCastill*)

Abbie picks up a needle
(*By courtesy of the* Sunday Express)

Lulu, three-year-old elephant

*Photographs not otherwise acknowledged
are from the author's collection*

Acknowledgements

The author gratefully acknowledges help given by: The Dogs' Home, Battersea Park Road, London SW8. Esso Petroleum Company Ltd, Victoria Street, London SW1. International Society for the Protection of Animals, 106 Jermyn Street, London SW1. Royal Society for the Prevention of Cruelty to Animals, 105 Jermyn Street, London SW1. Ministry of Public Buildings and Works (Royal Parks Division), Great Peter Street, London SW1. Curator, Household Cavalry Museum, Windsor. Reindeer Council of the United Kingdom, Newton Hill, Harston, Cambridge.

Introduction

All the stories in this book are true in every detail. They are as varied as the animals themselves but all of them illustrate the fact that we so often underrate the intelligence of our pets. We expect some reaction from the more domestic animals but are surprised when other creatures show appreciation and gratitude for what has been done for them. Basically, the role of a pet of any kind lies in the devotion and the complete reliance it places upon us, which, of course, flatters the human ego.

It will be evident that I have no special knowledge of animals, nor indeed is any such claim made. It will be obvious, however, that I have a love and respect for them and feel that man owes them a debt for the loyalty, companionship, interest and colour that they can bring into our workaday world.

Few pet lovers will read these pages without thinking that they themselves have a story, perhaps even more remarkable than some that appear here. If so, please let me know about them. Almost certainly I shall be writing a second volume at a later date.

I would like to take this opportunity of thanking all who have been so helpful when I have been seeking confirmation of stories, and also all who have been so accommodating when I have asked if I might go and see for myself.

E.R.D.

Penshurst
Exmouth
Devon, 1970

Man's Debt
to the Animal World

This is a book about animals. Some of them are servants of man, others are domestic pets, some are familiar to us, and others are more rarely seen. It has been said that Britain is as close to an earthly paradise for animals as any place on earth, and certainly there are in these islands, at a reasonable estimate, 6,000,000 cats, 5,000,000 dogs, and 8,000,000 birds kept as pets. By far the greater majority are well kept and much loved.

This abiding love of animals by the British is a strange phenomenon, emphasized by the legacies left to the Royal Society for the Prevention of Cruelty to Animals – a total of £833,965 in 1968, whilst the National Society for the Prevention of Cruelty to Children was left £421,250. (Income from other sources for the RSPCA was £537,877 and the NSPCC £767,656.) Little wonder that people of other nations find this hard to understand: and some will ponder over the fact that of the two societies it is the animals' which has received the Royal accolade.

The type of affection shown to animals varies widely, of course. Some people are maudlin about them, and will let pets become their masters or mistresses. In most cases, however, people are fond of the animals and grow to respect their personalities, without becoming their slaves. Families certainly find a household pet is a binding link.

Most pet owners seem to have a built-in belief that they understand their animal absolutely, but this is surely wishful thinking. The longer most of us spend with animals, the more we realize that we have little real knowledge of them. For days or weeks they will react in a certain way to a given set of circumstances and then suddenly, as if they had reasoned it was time for a change, they go off on a completely different tack. Of course, the various species have their own characteristics. A dog is usually eager to please: if it breaks a rule, then it will keep its distance till all is forgiven, or it will slither up and woo forgiveness, using its eyes like a film star. A cat, on the other hand, conveys definitely enough that it is standing no nonsense from a two-legged animal: 'You will come round before I do' – and it is generally right.

Dogs

The history of the dog in Britain is a long one. Sheepdogs and hunting dogs are familiar enough, but less well known is the fact that it was not until an Act of 1855, just over a hundred years ago, that it became illegal to use them as draught animals. Until then, harnessed to carts, they worked for a variety of people, mostly small tradesmen who could not afford a horse. Strange to say, one of the chief arguments for thus prohibiting the use of dogs was that they were used by sneak thieves who found them conveniently silent.

The shepherd's dog shows amazing intelligence, and incidents repeatedly occur which baffle us. In Scotland, a sheepdog recently broke away from his master, crossed a wide stream and, reaching the far side, began to round up some sheep. The mystery was that the sheep were on another farmer's land and in no way within the dog's domain. The dog, having got the sheep into a compact mass, proceeded to cut out six of them and herd them back across the stream. The action was completely incomprehensible until the shepherd recognized his own mark on the fleeces of the animals. No one had sent the dog to retrieve them, no one knew the sheep had become mixed, no one had missed them!

Such dogs are more than a right hand to their owners. They work incredibly hard and, but for their energy and endurance in covering forty miles or more a day, it would be difficult to prevent sheep from wandering far afield in the wild mountainous areas of Scotland, Wales and the Lake District. No striking for shorter hours or easier conditions, the dogs work from morning to night in all weathers, expecting nothing in return except their food and an occasional word of encouragement.

The guard or security dogs used by the police and others are further examples of a very high degree of intelligence. They even give their lives in their dangerous calling. In the public mind, perhaps the ultimate example of devoted and unselfish service to mankind is the guide dog for the blind. There are, however, many other specialists, like the huskies who serve men so faithfully in the Arctic regions.

There are instances every day of dogs that are just pets, but show an amazing intelligence and loyalty to their owners. One rescues a small boy from a fire, another a boy from drowning, and in numerous cases dogs give warning of imminent danger. Dogs will of their own accord attach themselves to children, watching over them like a mother. Then there are the sheer exhibitionists, dogs that smoke a pipe, drink beer, become vegetarians or something equally out of keeping, though nothing can equal the poor dog that went into space orbit. The story is told in these pages of how a Jack Russell terrier, of her own accord, took on the onerous task of watching successive clutches of ducklings immediately they were hatched.

The greatest attribute so far as man is concerned is probably the fact that a dog never, never grows away from him and leads a life of its own. In fact the older it gets the greater becomes its devotion. The dog has been described as man's first friend. Certainly no animal works so hard for so little reward.

Moreover, few would disagree with the statement that no two dogs are exactly alike in character. They are as different as the members of the human race. Each one works out his own set of duties, and usually the dog defines with patient persistence what he considers the best for his master or mistress. Even the most placid pet seems to have a built-in dislike of postmen and refuse-collectors. But, when one thinks of it, both these men carry a bag or a bin – they arrive, make a comparatively short visit and never, never are admitted to the house, as is perhaps a tradesman. Really, the dog's attitude would seem to be very clever reasoning.

Cats

Then there are the cats. It would be difficult to say how many elderly and lonely people would be completely alone, lost and despondent without their cat. Cats have personalities, they were the emblems of the earliest civilizations. In Ancient Rome the cat was a symbol of liberty; in Egypt it was held in great veneration, and whoever killed one, even by accident, was punished by death.

A cat loves its comfort, is selfish beyond description, incorrigibly inquisitive, sparing with its favours, and inclined to treat the whole human race with disdain. Its tactics in getting its own way are amusing. Disoblige a cat in any way, then watch it sit down and unconcernedly perform miracles of contortion while it washes itself, all the time obviously thinking out the next move. Nothing in this world compares with its elegant postures, the way it can relax and its meticulous cleanliness. There are, of course, working cats, mousers and ratters, there are those that keep down the pests in fisheries – and plenty that turn their hunting instinct to catching birds. A new classification is that of television entertainers. Nevertheless, be they farm cats, alley cats, Persian or Siamese, they have a character and personality all their own.

Considering they have been with us for a thousand years, we know little about them. Even in the quest for knowledge they defy us. Ignorance has led to the growth of a deal of nonsense and legend about them: a cat's reputed nine lives consist of no more nor less than a magnificently developed sense of preservation.

Their habits are mostly endearing, particularly the contented purr they can muster when things are just right: a German zoologist has advanced the theory that it is a means of communication, similar to the friendly smile of a human. Be that as it may, cats give every impression of fully appreciating the stupidity of man and of having arrived at a decision centuries ago that they would never bow to his will. What is more, they never have.

Horses

Horses have been friends and workmates of man for centuries; the love shown them is no new thing. In the fifteenth century the body of one worthy fighting man was brought back from the wars in Europe to be buried in a Cotswold church. In compliance with his last wish that he should not be parted from his favourite charger, he was buried with only the width of the chancel wall dividing him and his horse in death. Police horses have their own place in these pages; their dignity and poise during scenes of mob violence sets humanity in a poor light.

Ponies

Distinct from horses are ponies, many of which run wild in Britain until they are rounded up for annual sales. On Exmoor, Dartmoor and in the New Forest, there are comparatively large populations. The mealy-mouthed Exmoor pony has no counterpart; the whitish colouring round the muzzle and its wide chest make it immediately identifiable amongst all other ponies in the world. Records show that there were wild horses on Dartmoor before the Norman Conquest, and the true Dartmoor pony breed has descended from them.

Ponies, of course, are in great demand as children's pets, as most of the 2,000 or so horse shows and gymkhanas which take place annually in Britain will demonstrate. Man, however, is above all indebted to the ponies which for generations worked in the coal mines. Until 1842, women and girls had worked in the mines, the women particularly pushing and pulling the tubs of coal. In that year an Act of Parliament forbade such employment and ponies took over. Up to 1914, over 70,000 were used in Britain's collieries but their number was gradually reduced to half by 1937. Since then the increase in mechanization has been speeded up.

Up to the end of the nineteenth century the welfare of such animals was very much left to chance, but after 1911 they were carefully protected and well looked after. Their working life is between ten and fifteen years. Now they are being released. Members of the public making application to give them homes have to fulfil the most stringent conditions before the ponies may pass into private ownership. By 1971 none will be required to live lives underground. There are now less than 1,500 employed there.

Other Animals

In this book there are true stories about the resourcefulness and character of rabbits, donkeys, cows, goats, wild cattle, deer, squirrels and even a goose, swan, badger, tiger cubs and many others. Man may not be able to make them all into comforting pets, or make them work for him as does a sheep-dog or a horse, but he can get enormous pleasure from watching their ways. Perhaps more important, in learning about them he may learn something useful about himself.

Wild Birds in a Cage

One of the most vile types of cruelty is surely the capturing of wild birds by various methods, including the use of bird lime. The practice unfortunately still seems to flourish in some areas, and the mind boggles at the insensitivity of men who can take these beautiful wild things and sentence them to a life of imprisonment, probably in a cage only a foot square.

When a London café was raided, eighty-six birds were found, including finches, linnets, tree pipits, sparrows and bramblings. They had been in a cage for six days. They were in a terrible state with twenty-six either dead or dying. The other sixty were released and soared away to freedom. The five men who had trapped them, for sale as pets, were fined a total of £55.

The Things They Do

Fluffy the Fisherman

Time and again animals demonstrate that the exception often proves the rule. Cats, for instance, are said to hate water, and to go to any lengths to avoid it. An example of the other extreme was Fluffy, a Persian cat owned by Miss L. Dickenson, who lives on St Mary's in the Isles of Scilly.

Fluffy was a cat who loved fishing, and to reach her favourite vantage point she would wade into the water and then strike out quite strongly for the rocks. Once there, she would take up her position and, with typically cat-like patience and inscrutability, would watch and wait. Suddenly – whoosh – her paw would lash out, hooking her prey.

Like all good fishermen, Fluffy liked to bring home her spoils. So, grasping the fish firmly in her mouth, she would slip off the rocks into the sea, and swim back to the beach, all the while keeping a tight hold on her catch. Then she would make her way home, proudly deposit the fish upon the kitchen table, and wait to receive her due quota of praise. The suggestion that she should 'go and catch another one' always pleased her and she would be off like a flash to repeat her performance. Fluffy created several records. In one night she caught seven fish and her largest prize ever was a beautiful $1\frac{1}{2}$ lb plaice.

Sometimes she would deign to allow herself to be brought home in state, wrapped in a headscarf and cradled in the arms of some visitor, who had recognized Fluffy even in her soaking wet condition.

On the days when fishing did not appeal, Fluffy would swim to one of the boat anchorages, climb up on to the mooring, clean herself in leisurely fashion and then settle down comfortably to survey her kingdom. Satisfied that everything was in order, she would, in her own good time, make the return journey.

When Miss Dickenson took her dogs along the cliffs for a walk, the cat would always join the party.

Alas, one night this inveterate fisherman arrived home with a broken leg and, in spite of all the vet could do, it was considered kinder to put her to sleep.

Abbie Collects her Pay Packet

Many of us would cherish a companion as tidy-minded as Abbie, but Abbie, a Golden Labrador supplied by the Guide Dogs for the Blind Association, is doubly valuable to her owner, Miss M. Maclachlan, who has lost her sight.

Every day Abbie escorts her mistress to the Glasgow factory where she is employed as a telephonist. It is a journey which involves catching two buses, and which is repeated unerringly day after day, often in the face of confusing difficulties. One morning, whilst the dog and her mistress waited at the bus stop, a heavy vehicle drew up just beyond them. Miss Maclachlan tried to urge Abbie onto what she thought was her bus, but Abbie refused to move and continued to sit still and gaze in the direction from which she knew the bus would come.

On arrival at the factory her mistress goes to work in the

telephone room and the dog retires to a bed in a corner of the office. If this were all, it would be nothing remarkable, merely the work of most trained guide dogs. Over the years, however, Abbie has proved herself highly intelligent in a score of other ways and seems to know the most useful services she can render to her blind mistress, sensing the things which Miss Maclachlan finds it impossible to do for herself. When they arrive at the office, for instance, Abbie assumes her quiet office personality. If someone knocks at the door she lifts her head to see who it is, but remains placidly in her bed. This is very different from her behaviour if someone knocks on the door at home, for then she rushes out barking frantically and, should it prove to be friend, enthusiastically produces one of her toys for inspection. The office window-cleaner gets no attention other than a casual glance, but the window-cleaner at home is followed from room to room with a great display of ferocity.

On pay days, Abbie only has to hear the word 'wages' and she is off, making her way through the factory to the pay office. She collects the envelope and brings it back. On another day she takes the necessary coins and trots off to obtain her own box of cod liver oil capsules, infallibly returning with the change if there is any.

The amazing thing, however, is the way this animal has developed the picking up of small items to a delicate art. She will retrieve even a wet paint brush and place it carefully, handle first, into her owner's hand. Sometimes her mistress drops her purse and the money scatters all over the floor – every piece will be found, even sixpences. But perhaps Abbie's greatest feat is to pick up a needle and gently replace it, blunt end first, between her mistress' fingers without pricking her. A retrieved postage stamp only needs its gum renewing. Very often the first that Miss Maclachlan knows about a missing button is when the dog picks it up and noses it back into her hand.

Abbie is in fact fanatically tidy. One day she gently handed her mistress the tiny glass stopper and brush from a nail-varnish bottle which had been left 'untidily' in the hearth by a friend. On another occasion, a workman in Miss Maclachlan's flat needed a smaller screwdriver. One was supplied from the tool drawer but immediately it was finished with, Abbie picked it up and replaced it in the drawer.

Abbie's daily activities start when the alarm clock rings in the morning. She immediately gets out of her own bed and waits by her mistress' until she is assured that the bell has been heard and switched off. Then she goes back to bed until it is time to go downstairs. One morning, before Abbie had a chance to leave her bed, her owner assured her that she had heard the bell. Like many humans, grateful for that extra five minutes, Abbie turned over and snuggled down contentedly. Many people who have seen the dog believe she understands almost all the conversation going on around her. Now nine years old, she is still young both in activity and outlook. When playtime begins, she enters fully into the spirit of the game, but, when told to replace the ball or toy in the drawer, she knows the fun is over and, moving delicately as always, puts it back. Miss Maclachlan talks to her as she would to a human, and asserts that her whole life has been changed since this four-footed guardian entered her life.

A Self-appointed Mother

High up over the Exe valley, near Tiverton in Devon, is a hill farm where a farmer's daughter, Miss Eunice Middleton, rears Aylesbury ducklings. When they are hatched, the strangest of nursemaids, Rascal, a nine-year-old Jack Russell terrier bitch, takes over. From the time she first saw ducklings she became self-appointed foster-mother, nursemaid and watchdog.

As soon as each fresh batch of newly-hatched ducklings is placed in Rascal's basket, the terrier is most assiduous in her duties. She noses her charges over to get into her basket, then licks them and generally keeps order. She nestles in with them and woe betide any unauthorized being who comes near. The cats particularly are not allowed even a long view. Certainly the diminutive balls of yellow fluff seem to adore the terrier.

At night, Rascal sleeps at the foot of her mistress' bed, but at least three times during the night she dutifully trots downstairs to inspect her charges. Rascal was never taught to do this. Perhaps it is her maternal instinct asserting itself, for she has never had pups of her own and simply seems to want something to guard and fuss over. For some years now she has mothered successive batches of chicks, numbering anything up to 200 a season.

Rascal is also a splendid guard dog, with a number of tricks in her repertoire, but none so strange as this unusual manifestation of the maternal instinct.

Taffy the Regimental Goat

When the Royal Regiment of Wales (formerly the 24/41st Foot) goes on parade, by far the proudest member is the regimental mascot, Taffy the goat.

His natural coat is milky-white in colour and on parade his number one dress is a grass-green coat, with the regimental insignia embroidered in gold and silver. The points of his long horns have silver tips and on his forehead he wears a silver nameplate. No one knows his exact age, but he is probably about ten.

He can be uncooperative during rehearsals for parades or special ceremonies, but when the time comes and the band strikes up he invariably rises to the occasion, just as if he knows that the limelight is on him and that he must not let the side down.

Taffy comes from a long line of goats who have led the regiment, for the first such mascot was adopted during the Crimean War. The reason why a goat should have been chosen for the honour is obscure, but one called Billy was certainly present at the last stages of the siege of Sebastopol in 1855. He was with the regiment when it was inspected by Queen Victoria on its return from the Crimean campaign, retired with honour, and lived until 1861. He was succeeded by another of the species who served and died in the West Indies. Successors were presented to the regiment by various people included a Sultan, Queen Victoria and the Duke of Wellington. In 1895, however, the Duke's goat was attacked by another and was killed in the battle which followed. The usurper then reigned in his stead.

So the present Taffy has something to live up to. He is descended from a herd of Kashmir goats, established at Windsor in 1828. The herd, in which the Prince Consort took a personal interest, must have been quite a large one, for at one time over 1,000 people were engaged in making shawls from their fine wool. In 1936, King Edward VIII presented ten goats from the herd to the London Zoo, and since then the mascots of the Welch Regiment have been drawn from there.

In 1969 the regiment mounted guard at Buckingham Palace, taking over from the Irish Guards. This was quite an occasion for, whilst Taffy led the Welch Regiment, Seahan, the Wolfhound mascot of the Irish Guards, was also on parade. There was much conjecture as to how the goat and the dog would behave when confronted with each other. In the event there was no need to worry. Both animals carried out their parts with great dignity and obvious mutual disdain.

This dignity stood Taffy in good stead when the Colonel-in-Chief, the Prince of Wales, performed his first military duty in presenting new colours at the regiment's inauguration parade at Cardiff Castle. Taffy was also on parade at the Investiture of the Prince of Wales in 1969.

Taffy, like all his predecessors, was trained from an early age by the regiment's goat major for the part he would eventually play. Already he must surely be the most travelled goat in the world, having served with the regiment in Hong Kong and in Germany. His predecessor had one vice, an insatiable craving for tobacco, but so far Taffy is content with one or two cigarettes a day and these he chews with relish. Given the opportunity, however, he will eat anything, and has special fondness for a particular breakfast cereal. But Taffy is far too valuable for his diet not to be carefully controlled.

Playmates Unlimited

For years past in Harrogate, Yorkshire, Jack, a taxi-driver's dog, has amused many and pestered some, by his trick of getting someone to play with him.

Jack accompanies his master to work every day and makes his base at the drivers' shelter at the taxi-rank on the edge of the Stray, an open space. When his master goes off with his first fare, Jack has his morning snooze and then wakes up wanting his exercise. The fact that there is no other dog to play with does not worry him one bit; he goes to the nearest public bench, the type that seats about six people, and nudges in the back the first person that takes his fancy. Having thus gained attention, he trots round to the front and drops his ball at his chosen victim's feet. Usually the person responds, throwing it good-humouredly for Jack to retrieve, and that is his great mistake, for the game goes on and on and on. No rest is allowed and the human's only hope of relief is to walk away.

Jack then remains pensive for a while. One can almost feel him weighing up the possibilities of the people that are left. However, his selection made, by some formula known only to himself, he repeats his routine. First a nudge in the back, then the presentation of the ball, and off the game goes once more.

Sometimes the bench is empty; but Jack knows the answer to that one. Far too wise to sit too near, he retires to the foot of a tall tree within sight of the seats, and, pretending to sleep, keeps perpetual vigilance. Strange to say, he does not jump forward to the first person who sits down. It seems he or she has to pass his personal test, and that once the person with the necessary qualifications pauses to rest, Jack goes over to make acquaintance. Rarely does he make a bad choice, and almost always his chosen playmate responds.

Jack is as adamant about his territorial rights as he is about making people play. Four public paths cross his area, and when a dog running free comes near, Jack puts on an act of ferocious barking. If, on the other hand, the trespassing dog is on a lead, he is magnificently ignored.

Jack is an institution now in that part of Harrogate and a continual source of interest to people nearby – particularly those watching from a safe distance!

Age Twenty-six . . . Twenty-one Children

Blackie has retired. For twenty-six years she has given of her bovine best, a best that has included twenty-one calves and upwards of 20,000 gallons of milk. Moreover, not once in her twenty-six years has she given her owner cause for concern or ever received medical attention.

A Friesian cross, she was a war baby, born in 1943 at Brayley Barton in North Devon, and year after year her milk yield exceeded 1,000 gallons. Normally farmers are happy about a cow that still gives milk at twelve years of age, but Blackie at twice that age was continuing to keep pace with the younger cows. Blackie's owner, farmer Mr Michael Paine, asserts she is a once-in-a-lifetime cow and estimates that she has earned him more than £4,000.

Now Blackie is receiving a generous reward for her unstinting service, has retired with full honours and is allowed to roam about the farm at will. Whilst this is justice, it is nevertheless extremely rare for the master of a humble cow to show appreciation in such a way. Usually when cows have finished their productive life, they are put down – this story indeed has a happy ending.

Seven-thousand-to-one Chance

Calf triplets are rare – their rate of occurrence being considered as one in 7,000 births. They are even less likely to survive, but Doreen, a handsome Friesian cow on a farm at Shebbear, again in North Devon, had three splendid little calves, and all lived.

Mrs M. Metherell, the farmer's wife, hand-fed them for a while, and soon they were romping round the farm, as fine a trio as could be. At birth they weighed fifty-six, sixty-four and sixty-nine pounds respectively. One of them was a bull, and it was his fate to leave the family circle, but the two heifers are now a year old.

Doreen is one of twenty cows on the farm, and she has

always been a favourite. Up to the time of the birth, she was yielding some six gallons of milk a day.

The last time there was such an event on the farm was at the turn of the century, and on that occasion not all the youngsters survived.

The Dog who Went to Church

Of all animals, the dog has certainly had a chequered career throughout the centuries, at least so far as social acceptability is concerned. In the seventeenth century there were so many in and around villages, where they acted as scavengers, that measures had to be taken to keep them out of the churches, and for this purpose many church authorities appointed a dog whipper. As recently as 1969, Southwell Minster in Nottinghamshire advertised such a post, though it is true that the modern duties included everything but the original one. A notice displayed in a Scottish church in the mid-seventeenth century proclaimed:

Every man that brings dogges to the kirk with them to pay 40 shillings for the first tym a mark for the second tym whilk is still to be doublet so long as they continue so doing.

As late as the nineteenth century, however, in rural areas where farmers and farmworkers travelled some distance to attend church, their dogs were allowed to enter and lie quietly under the pews while the service was in progress.

The air raids during World War II caused another dog to be taken to church, and led to his successors having the same privilege. It happened like this. When the Reverend Cecil Curwen was vicar of All Saints, Surrey Square, London, he had a crossbred Labrador spaniel named Chum. During a daylight raid in September 1940, the vicarage received a direct hit; fortunately the vicar was not injured although the roof had gracefully subsided down the side of the house. As he was being got out, Mr Curwen let his rescuers know that there was a dog in the house, and someone went in and found Chum quite uninjured in the space between the wall of the house and the roof. Very shortly afterwards, the church itself was hit by a bomb, and from then on the dog accompanied his master wherever he went. The church hall was next to be destroyed, and services were then held in the cellar of a neighbouring vicarage. It was here that Chum, who in the raids was frightened but never panic-stricken, found his own air-raid shelter – under the temporary altar. Raid followed raid in that part of London, and Chum and his master had a number of narrow escapes, but wherever the vicar went his dog accompanied him.

When the war was over, Mr Curwen became vicar of St Clements in the City Road, and it was at this period that Chum died. His successor was Blaize, a cocker spaniel, and he was trained to go to church and lie quiet. In due course Blaize died and the vicar's present companion, Rex, a yellow Labrador, soon became in his turn a model church-goer. During weekday services he would take his place by the altar at the vicar's new church of All Souls, Brighton, and at Mass on Sundays he would sit in the nave. After services, he would walk up and down greeting the congregation, with most of whom he was a firm favourite. When his master removed to another living at Hove, Rex was not a bit put out; he simply carried on as he had left off.

Now the vicar has retired and Rex is getting old and suffers from rheumatism, but he still attends any service his master conducts.

Pepper the Church-goer

There is a very different story to be told abut Pepper, a fine ginger tom-cat belonging to the landlady of a village inn. Pepper decided he liked the look of the new vicar and took up church-going. Every morning he would follow the vicar to church and sometimes he went alone. On occasions he would get shut in, and in his efforts to find a way out he often left footprints all over the altar linen.

Now Pepper's seven-year stint of church-going is over; he has been banned from the thirteenth-century church of Stoke-in-Teignhead in South Devon. In time-honoured fashion, a notice was posted on to the door:

A cat has been making himself a nuisance in the Church, so please keep the door closed.

Pepper's owner has two other cats, but they are not religious fanatics, keeping well away from the church and the church-yard. What other haunt poor Pepper will find is anybody's guess.

Chick Collects Golf Balls

Maung Putzi is the aristocratic name of a brown Burmese cat. Except for the fact that as a kitten he had to be nursed through feline enteritis, and later escaped death when a piano fell on him, the first two years of his life were relatively un-eventful. But who knows what psychosis inhibited Chick (for that is his everyday name) for that period.

Suddenly he adopted a new routine. Leaving his garden, he would make his way through the rough undergrowth which edged the adjoining golf course, and there lie in wait. His vantage point was close to the seventeenth hole. As the players approached and took their shot for the hole, Chick would pounce. He cared not one bit whether the ball was rolling straight and true to hole in one or even two or three – if the ball was a new one, that was all this Burmese marauder asked. While the ball was still in motion, he would dart on to the fairway, gather it up in his mouth and run for home, where he would proudly carry it into the kitchen.

For ten months Chick played this particular brand of golf. His owner, Mrs Harris of Redditch, Worcestershire, took little notice to start with. When she saw him playing with his first golf ball, she thought he had picked it up in the garden, and that it had probably been hit there by an over-enthusiastic golfer.

Soon, however, noticing the frequency of his game, and finding a well-worn track through the long grass, she discovered the true reason. On average, a dozen balls a week were brought home. And they were mostly good ones, for Chick was fastidious and did not much care for dirty or split specimens. The Harrises were embarrassed but there was nothing much they could do about it. Another member of the household, Chick's mother, Vicky, scorns to hunt anything that is not alive and kicking.

Alas, not only dogs have their day, and Chick's Nemesis arrived when the family moved to a house far away and nowhere near a golf course. Now Chick lies in the sun and dreams of the days when his enthusiasm for collecting golf balls rivalled a human collector's urge for, say, antiques – or money.

Bill the Badger

A Forest of Dean gamekeeper found a baby badger huddled up against its dead mother, rescued the little fellow, and in due course gave him to Mr and Mrs P. Gaskell, who live in Wimpstone, some four and a half miles from Stratford-on-Avon. Promptly christened Bill by the Gaskell's two daughters Rebecca and Rosanna, he settled in with them so comfortably that he now is as regular in his habits as a bowler-hatted commuter.

For the first twelve months Bill roamed the house by day in much the same way as a cat or dog would do, except that he showed no inclination to go out, other than when the family went for a walk across the fields. In that case, not wanting to be left behind, he ambled along with them. But as night crept on, Bill changed gear. At 8 o'clock precisely, he put his no mean weight against the back door to let everyone know it was time for his nocturnal prowl. Then off he went on his own adventures, but without fail returned at 7 o'clock next morning, another bang on the door advising the family that he wanted to come in.

When he grew older, however, he went out one day and dug himself a sett under a hollow elm tree in the garden, some 200 or 300 yards from the house. Now he spends most of the day sleeping there. But his built-in alarm clock still operates, for at 8 PM precisely he leaves his sett, goes to the kitchen door and lets the family know that he is off. Never, ever, does he disappear on his nightly jaunt without first notifying them. He repeats the performance when he returns in the morning.

Whilst Bill is happy to spend time with the family, he does not take kindly to visitors. If someone arrives when he is in the house, he takes himself off and settles comfortably in the bottom of a wardrobe until the coast is clear again. Mrs Gaskell feels certain he will never lose his wariness and natural caution.

Bill will play with the children and in spite of his undoubted strength never harms them, but he is far too rough for the dogs in the house. Now he weighs forty pounds and is two years old. The family know a lot about him – except what he gets up to at night. That is Bill's own closely guarded secret.

Digger – Australian Tough Guy

To adopt a stray in Australia and then, because it was unmanageable, pay $200 to send it 12,000 miles by air as a VIP passenger to England, is quite something, even in the annals of the dog-loving fraternity. This was, however, what actually happened to Digger, a black cross spaniel, and he must be one of the luckiest, as well as one of the pluckiest, dogs alive. The full story is best told by the person concerned, Miss Val Lowe, who emigrated to Sydney from Margate, Kent:

I first met up with Digger about three years ago when I was employed as a window-dresser at a store in the Sydney suburb of Compsie. At that time, the registration of dogs in this State had just been made compulsory and it was a common sight to see packs of abandoned dogs roaming the streets.

One little black dog in particular soon became a familiar sight hanging around the doors of the store. Obviously hungry, he still had a somewhat jaunty air about him which was immediately attractive. Being a soft touch, I suppose, I bought him an occasional tin of meat which was quickly dispatched. Suddenly after a few days he disappeared and I concluded that he had gone the way of most stray dogs, with the local dog-catchers!

However, some days later there he was again. This time in a pathetic condition, thin, one paw held in the air. Too much for me, I'm afraid! Against all practical reasoning, that night he was on his way home with me on the train.

A visit to the vet confirmed that he had an abscess in his paw, that he had 'rotten old teeth', and that he had had distemper as a pup. Not really a very good proposition as a dog! He was identified as a cross kelpie-spaniel. With this dingo ancestry the obvious name for him was Digger.

It soon became obvious that Digger loved all humans, and indoors he was a real pet. Once outside, though, Jekyll became Hyde. Strangely, for all his previous wanderings, he had no road sense at all; a motor-cycle would produce a barking frenzy, and the sight of another dog would turn him into a tear-away thug. Dogs big or small, he would take them all on, with no qualms about tackling even an Alsatian. His daily walks became a nightmare and a source of continual embarrassment. He became the terror of the harbourside park, which was nearest my flat. Other owners would promptly vanish round the nearest corner when Digger appeared. I have a vivid recollection of his seizing an unfortunate white poodle, who gradually changed in colour from white to grey to black as he was hauled through the mud, while his hysterical female owner broke her folding umbrella on Digger's head.

He could swim like a beaver, his favourite targets being the various ornamental pools in the vicinity. Once he nearly gave me heart failure by jumping into the harbour and swimming out until his head was a black dot in the distance, when he was whistled back by a kindly stranger.

As time went on it became obvious that keeping Digger cooped up in a flat was doing him no good at all. We were both becoming neurotic. What to do with him?

Hopefully I advertised in the local paper. One reply only, for a guard dog, convinced me that this was not the solution. After a while the idea of sending him home to my parents took root. It was a big step but fortunately I have a friend who works for an international airline. He was able to make the whole idea feasible, even to the extent of arranging a concession fare.

So one morning a little later Digger left for England. I could not go to the airport but my friend reported that his last sight of Digger was of his jaunty flag of a tail still wagging as he was conveyed to the waiting 'V' jet.

Of course, it meant six months quarantine before he was finally turned over to my parents. Not that they were particularly keen to take him, even though they had just lost their pedigree Golden Retriever. However, gamely, they agreed. So Digger arrived in Margate.

Although the garden of the Lowes' home at Margate is a large one, it was not big enough for Digger. It just became a prison camp for him, with himself as the star escaper. The fence was built higher and higher, but still he managed to escape. On one occasion he was brought back in style from three miles away in a motorized invalid carriage.

Then Miss Lowe's parents sent him to a correction school, but this had no effect whatsoever. Finally, in desperation, they sent him to be neutered, and that operation did have some effect, though not quite in the way intended – after a few weeks he put on so much weight that try as he might he could not jump over the fence.

Digger is now four and a half years old and seems in some measure to have accepted his fate. He is still an affectionate pet indoors, but scowls at motor-cycles and other dogs through the front window, and often, by his faraway look, gives the impression that he is running with the wild dingo pack, probably leading them far, far away.

Any boy who behaved like Digger would probably be given every benefit of the doubt. It would be pleaded that he had had a broken home, and that unless society did something for him he would finish up a delinquent. Who knows what happened to Digger in his puppyhood?

Miss Lowe and her parents have certainly given Digger the benefit of the doubt, and even if a delinquent, he has courage, quick wits and, at bedrock, lots of affection for those who have been so good to him.

Arthur Captivates the Judge

Not every cat can receive the full measure of glamour which surrounds a television personality, and if Arthur could have worked it out for himself, he would probably, like many people in public life, have wondered whether it was worth it.

Arthur, with his beautiful white fur, had for a long time decorated a television commercial by scooping out his so-called favourite food from a tin. The delicate way in which he did this with his paw was greatly admired. He had many other publicity assignments too; then a legal battle erupted as to his ownership and the whole of Arthur's life was subjected to the glare of the spotlight. Poor Arthur! The food he ate, his particular preference for soft foods, his not liking other cats and kittens, his alleged unsociability, in fact his whole personality lay exposed.

During the case, Arthur was taken to the High Court in a white cage and placed in a lawyer's consulting room to await 'call'. Then, with a lead attached to his gold collar, he was taken into the court and put on the Judge's bench. He even suffered the indignity of having his mouth examined to determine the condition of his teeth. Before leaving the court, the

Judge tickled him under the chin and Arthur promptly signalled his appreciation by purring loudly. Another tickle and then came the pronouncement that he could be released. It is not every day that a cat appears at the Courts of Justice. It is not every day that a cat is tickled by a judge.

Faithful to the End

Idol was a pedigree Alsatian. He was born on 16th October, 1965, and from the age of six months lived with Police Constable Shepherd and his
family. In due course his
master, a dog handler and a
member of the Surrey Constabulary, took him to an
elementary training course
for dogs at the constabulary
headquarters, where he acquitted himself very well.
He then went on to an advanced course, which he
passed with flying colours, to
be classed as 'operational'.

Idol entered into his new job with zest, and very soon became an expert. He was responsible for one arrest after another, until the total reached twenty-five. Other assignments came his way, too – he found a missing child and also played no small part in the recovery of a considerable amount of stolen property.

Then, in 1969, just after his fourth birthday, tragedy struck. Police Constable Shepherd and a colleague were called to a break-in at a community centre at Egham and eventually a man with a double-barrelled shotgun appeared.

Crouching behind bushes, the man held the police at bay in front of the building for almost two hours, threatening to shoot if anyone approached. The policemen were using a police vehicle as a shield and it was then that his handler sent Idol at the man. The dog approached and, as he got reasonably close, paused. At that moment the man raised his gun and fired at the animal, wounding him so severely that he had to be destroyed. Immediately the shot was fired, the police pounced and captured the man.

In the police-dog training manual, emphasis is placed on teaching a dog to stand off when and so long as the suspect stands still. Idol meticulously obeyed the rule and only went in when the gunman raised his weapon, but it was too late. Idol maintained the highest traditions of his kind at the cost of his own life.

Every year British police dogs make between 1,000 and 2,000 arrests, more or less unaided. One wonders how many human lives are thereby saved.

They Share a Coat of Arms

Bimbo, a rhesus monkey, made front-page news when she escaped from a cage at London's Heathrow Airport after arriving in this country. Just as with people, there are animals which never regard prison bars as escape-proof. Bimbo played a waiting game and then, when opportunity presented itself, led four of her companions in a break-out after making a hole in the wire mesh of their cage.

Her fellow escapees had not a tithe of Bimbo's skill at evading capture, and all too soon they were back behind bars. Not so Bimbo. For seven months she successfully pitted her animal wits against all that humans and their various aids could do. Many men have been known to receive an award for less spectacular feats.

Possessing all the skill of an escapologist, Bimbo's tactics were extraordinary. In the cargo warehouse at the Airport she gleefully took the food that was laid as a bait, and swept gracefully from girder to girder. She would allow keepers to come quite close, then off she would leap, sometimes squatting on the top of her cage and sometimes on a tree just outside the warehouse, but always just out of reach.

Then a new ruse occurred to her. She would hop into her cage, then just as the poor humans thought they had her, would leap out quickly and outwit them once again. She did this several times, but all good things come to an end and she played the trick once too often. Even then the honours went to her, for it was only a drugged dart that eventually slowed her down.

Bimbo's owner is also the owner of Fred, a basset hound. Fred is another believer in the rights of the individual. One of the delights of his life was to take a morning stroll to Chessington Zoo where, with the aplomb of a season-ticket holder, he would whisk through the gates and go on a tour. But dogs are not allowed in the zoo and, although this particular one did no harm, rules are rules. Time after time the authorities had to telephone Fred's master and a chauffeur-driven Rolls-Royce would be sent to collect him.

At the time that Bimbo and Fred were in the news, their owner, the chairman of the National Research Development Corporation, was made a life peer; a coat-of-arms was granted to him as Lord Black of Barrow-in-Furness in the County Palatine of Lancaster. And these two animals – the basset hound and the rhesus monkey – were made the two supporters of the coat-of-arms, an unusual distinction. Both have shown zeal and a sense of purpose, so that the motto *Per Ardua* – by hard work – is a fitting tribute.

Ralph on the Retired List

Ralph has done his Army service and is now retired in every sense of the word. Like most veterans, he is enjoying what he has dreamed about for so long – a comfortable home life.

Ralph is a black and tan Alsatian. He is nine years of age and weighs ninety pounds, but he is no ordinary dog. For eight years he served in the Army as a security dog; he was fearless and, above all, was super-intelligent. Three times he qualified for the United Kingdom Dog Trials at Melton Mowbray, Leicestershire, and in 1968 won the obedience and agility trials at the Army's Strategic Command trials at Aldershot, Hampshire. In this gruelling test the dogs have to clear hurdles, crawl through tunnels, jump in and out of windows, cross slippery logs and perform all kinds of complicated manoeuvres. They are assessed for general obedience, intelligence and agility.

The following year he was again entered. Ralph knew the course and what he had to do, but rheumatism – that archenemy of all dogs who work outside in all weathers – was discernible in his gait. So he was put on the retired list, and a successor was given the task of guarding the secrets of the Army's Experimental Establishment at Shoeburyness.

Police Constable Tony Dibnah had been Ralph's handler since 1966; they had taken pride in their joint achievements. So when four-footed Private No B218 was to be retired, his handler asked if he could take him into civilian life. The Army agreed, and Ralph settled down with Tony Dibnah and his family. There are three children, Lorraine (13), Lyn (8) and David (3), and Ralph is as gentle as a lamb. He is adored by all the family; what more could a retired soldier want?

In his new surroundings Ralph soon worked things out for himself. For instance, he is not very fond of water to drink, much preferring tea or milk. Therefore, he is provided with two bowls, one for water and one for tea. The water is always there but if he feels like a cuppa, he fetches the tea bowl and puts it down in front of his master. Sometimes, however, he has an urge for milk, and then he goes and sits in front of the refrigerator.

Next Stop the Moon

All children hear about the cow that jumped over the moon. Yet most of us would be surprised if we saw a cow jump over even a small obstacle. Jennifer Robertson, daughter of a farmer in Argyllshire, finds nothing unusual about it, for her pet cow, Manda, jumps hurdles to order when being ridden.

Manda was singled out as a pet when she was a calf, and from the start raised little objection to being ridden, although she used to buck occasionally and her rider suffered many a fall. Then one day a small hurdle was erected and when Manda was ridden at it she cleared it gracefully. What is more she seemed to enjoy the experience. The height was increased to over two feet and she still took the hurdle in her stride.

This extraordinary animal is one of a herd of seventy Ayrshires, and the others show their disapproval of the whole act by butting her when she rejoins them after her point-to-point. But she takes this philosophically and they soon tire of it. Although both Manda's mother and grandmother have allowed themselves to be ridden, they have never aspired to jumping.

Manda obviously thinks that special treatment is her due, for if no one is looking she will nose open the sliding doors of the barn and get at the barley, which generally gives her hearty indigestion. Manda's equestrian act in no way affects her more normal function of producing milk.

Jennifer must indeed have a way with animals, for she trained a whole bunch of calves to jump over the feeding troughs when she clapped her hands. But they became far too proficient and she had to stop before they learnt to jump out of the yard, let alone over the moon!

A Rose by any other Name . . .

It used to be commonplace for sheep to be allowed to graze in the churchyard. The practice served the dual purpose of providing pasture for the sheep and a tidy churchyard for the parish, but in more sophisticated days, for some obscure reason, it came to be frowned upon. The man with a scythe, later with shears and even a lawnmower has taken over the sheep's duties. But now, with human labour scarce and expensive, sheep are having a come-back and their services are being eagerly sought, particularly in country districts, to keep the churchyards tidy.

It is rare, however, to see a billy-goat doing similar work, but a Londoner has turned his pet goat, Snowy, to lawnmowing and edge-trimming. It all came about when the owner's garden began to resemble a jungle through lack of attention. The task looked formidable, but not to Snowy. He set about the job with gusto and made a remarkably neat job of it in a short space of time. His master, who is trying to raise £150 for a guide dog for the blind, is now hiring out the goat to anybody who needs a part-time gardener. Among the assignments received has been one of clipping the grass and trimming round the gravestones in a cemetery. Snowy was a great success at this, and perhaps he has set a fashion. At any rate there is no rubbish to burn when he is on the job, for he eats it all.

Topsy's Journey

Goats frequently hit the headlines. They are useful animals in many circumstances, and in the Western Isles of Scotland they frequently provide the milk, for often the pasture is not good enough to keep a cow. It was for this purpose that Topsy, a fine goat, became involved in a 600-mile journey from Peterborough, in Northamptonshire, to the Isle of Skye.

A crofter was living at Point of Sleat, seven miles from any other village on Skye. His three little girls – Elsbeth, Emma and Morag – needed milk, and as they possessed no cow it was difficult to obtain. Then on the mainland, the crofter's friend Ian Holdsworthy saw a goat advertised for £10. He thought of the island family, and snapped it up. Then came the problem – how to transport his purchase all the way from Peterborough to Skye.

With the goat on a lead, and carrying a bag of hay as sustenance for the journey, Ian Holdsworthy bought a ticket at Peterborough railway station. Airily he explained his charge away as being an African mountain dog. The first change was at Grantham, where unfortunately Topsy forgot herself and butted a railway porter. The journey continued. At Fort William she was duly admired by other passengers, and at Mallaig, Inverness-shire, she was milked. Except for the one misdemeanour at Grantham, she was a perfect little lady and an ideal passenger. Eventually Ian Holdsworthy and his 'African mountain dog' took the ferry to Skye, and the long trip was over.

The three little girls were delighted to welcome Topsy even before they tasted her milk.

With Cat-like Tread

Another example of the inscrutable mystery of cat minds was demonstrated in a recent winter to a resident of Berkshire who owned five cats, a number swollen to seven by two pregnant visitors. Over the years the cats had trodden a long and clearly-defined cat-walk from one end of the garden to the other. It was by no means a straight path, rather a series of wiggles which the cats negotiated meticulously in their comings and goings.

Then came the winter and the snow. The cat-walk was hidden but still the cats traced their path unerringly, probably from habit. The amazing thing was that all seven cats trod in exactly the same footmarks as they went to and fro. The original footprints were made by the first of the cats to venture out into the white wilderness. It daintily picked its way along the unseen cat-walk, leaving four clearly defined prints with each step. During the day all the cats used the path at some time or another, and each one of them placed its paws with seeming ease exactly into the marks made by the first cat.

For six days the snow lasted and for six days there remained only the set of four prints made by the first cat, although all seven had used the path constantly. This would have been extraordinary even if all the cats had been of similar shape and size, but they were a well-assorted collection. Three of them were shortly to become mothers and one of them was very old. None of them made any apparent effort, none of them so much as glanced behind to locate the exact position for its back feet, yet none of them ever faltered.

Inborn Instinct

The way in which dogs of certain breeds show their hereditary traits at an early age is fantastic. This is particularly noticeable in sheepdogs such as Border collies.

One such, Dusky, born near a Cotswold farm, was collected at the age of three months by his new owner who lived near Exeter. Getting him back to Devonshire by car presented a few problems. The pup was small enough to be put into a cat basket, but he was obviously going to be a character and keeping him there was another story. His new boss was negotiating the steep gradient of Cleeve Hill, Cheltenham, when the pup decided he would like to make closer acquaintance; so he climbed out of the basket, scrambled over the seat and up on to the driver's shoulders. Pushed down, he then explored the floor of the car, made a puddle, curled up and went to sleep, in which blissful state he remained for the next three and a half hours, only waking when his new home was reached. He was soon very active and grew fast, travelling some 500 miles a week all over the country in the car with his master.

His first adventure with sheep took place on the wild Yorkshire moors beyond Hawes, when he was still very young. He was let out of the car for a stretch and within seconds was away. Right to the top of the moor he went, not pausing as he climbed the steep inclines to a height of about 250 feet. From the road he had spotted sheep running free on the hillside, and it was only a matter of minutes before he had rounded them up and was driving them before him. Fortunately his direction ran parallel with the road, so his bewildered owner drove along trying to keep level. Even at that early age he had been trained to return from short distances when the car hooter sounded – but this time he ignored the call. The thrill of the job was really in his blood. For about one and a half miles he drove the sheep in a compact mass and had a whale of a time. Then at last two sheep broke away and rushed down to the road. Dusky followed and was caught. The amazing thing is that he had never been face to face with a sheep before, let alone caught its scent.

His owner learnt later in the day that three dogs had been shot during the previous week for chasing sheep. Dusky could well have been the fourth.

Slow Rate of Growth

For more than 570 years Powderham Castle has occupied a position on the west bank of the River Exe in Devon. Some 250 deer roam at will in the magnificent park, where they are a constant delight to visitors.

Not so easily seen, or so beautiful or graceful, is Timothy the tortoise, who keeps himself to himself in the shrubbery at the foot of the ancient tower. He probably feels entitled to take things easy, for records show he is well over a hundred years old. Even more startling is the fact that, according to records which have been meticulously kept, Timothy has grown just one-eighth of an inch in the last ninety years.

Today, this old stager has company, though he does not seem to be very excited about it – a younger tortoise now shares the dry patch by the old castle. They do not quarrel over the odd lettuce leaf and, by their decorous behaviour, perhaps show humans that there is more in life than racing around saving time at all costs and then being at a loss usefully to employ the minutes saved by such exertions.

Scatt – Secret Agent

The eyes of secret agent 007 glittered as his body tensed, ready for the kill. Specially recruited to track down and destroy the mysterious enemy which was causing havoc at the Signals Research and Development Establishment, near Bournemouth, Hampshire, this young agent dispatched the enemy with speed and efficiency.

The trouble in question arose when it was discovered that underground cables relaying signals to space satellites were being savagely slashed. At one time it was suspected that enemy agents were at work but finally the real cause was discovered – a plague of rats.

Special agent 007, otherwise known as Scatt, is a handsome black cat, one of two kittens born in a nearby village. From his earliest days he showed signs of developing into a superb hunter and, when the crisis at the research station developed, it was decided that he was 'made' for the job. Within a day or two Scatt had proved his worth by smelling out and destroying the enemy. The problem of the cut cables ceased but Scatt remains on the strength of the establishment.

Like all military personnel he has to conform to the rules, and his uniform is a collar and lead on those occasions when he has to be on parade with his colleagues of the Royal Corps of Signals.

How did Rusty do it?

Rusty was a young sheepdog, owned by a Devonshire farmer,

formerly living at Slapton. He had always enjoyed the complete freedom of farm life, and when the family moved fifty miles across the country to Payhembury village, Rusty went too in the back of the car.

Because it was felt he was likely to wander in the settling-down period at his new home, he was confined until he could be taken out. But after a few days Rusty got out on his own and was off. The family searched for him in vain, until they heard from the police that he had arrived at their former home at Slapton.

It is difficult to imagine what happened on that lonely journey when he must have felt that every man's hand was against him. From Payhembury, he would probably have gone along the busy A30 road which in the season carries practically non-stop traffic, and even in the quieter months is always busy. Then as he approached Exeter, he would have felt confused, just as a country-born human being would be when faced with a city jungle for the first time. Nevertheless, somehow Rusty, by what trial and error, by what fruitless march and countermarch we shall never know, must have crossed the city and found himself on the A30 again, with the Torquay and the Plymouth traffic flashing by. Which way did he head then? Along the River Exe to Newton Abbot? Did he stick to the main road or did he perhaps keep to the byways until he struck his former home?

It is heart-breaking to think of the many bitter disappointments he must have experienced, of his many escapes from the traffic, of his search for food. How far did he really travel to cover that fifty miles – 100 or 200 miles? Many breeds of dogs can travel forty, even fifty miles in a day's work, but poor old Rusty took a fortnight. Only his dejected and physical condition on arrival can tell us a tiny part of the real story. He was wild, unkempt, very thin, and his pads were in a bad state.

When his owners were notified of his arrival, they collected him, overjoyed at his return to Payhembury. For just nine days he seemed content to be home, but he must have found the new non-farming life strange for suddenly he disappeared once more and, sad to say, was never heard of again.

The Collie Provided Proof

After many years of farming in the beautiful Gloucestershire countryside, a farmer retired and passed the farm on to his son. The young man was right up-to-date with tractors, harvesters and other machinery but he would have nothing to do with dogs, maintaining that they were overrated and that a man could bring in the sheep unaided.

When a neighbouring farmer who had hundreds of sheep also retired, he offered his black and white collie to the young farmer. The latter, perhaps because he was having second thoughts, or because he did not want to offend, accepted, and the dog took up his duties at the new farm.

The first week went well. At precisely the same time every day, the collie would trot off, round up the sheep a few fields away and bring them home. On the eighth day, however, the sheep arrived but the dog failed to come with them. The farmer, with bad grace, eventually went to look for him and, going to the field where the sheep had come from, found the dog sitting beside a sheep which was on its back and unable to right itself. Once the point that dogs know their duty and are prepared to do it in all circumstances had thus been made, he was accepted as a valuable addition to the working force of the farm, and, with his centuries-old instinct of looking after his charges come rain or shine, is worth any man.

Ross the Commando

A signal honour indeed was conferred upon Ross, a Golden Labrador, at the Infantry Training Centre, Royal Marines, Lympstone, near Exmouth. For having completed the very tough commando course, he was ceremonially awarded a green collar in place of the famous green commando beret.

Ross was originally intended to be a guide dog. He possessed all the necessary qualities but one – he would unfortunately fight other dogs. Rejected, therefore, at twelve months of age, he became the pet of Quartermaster-Sergeant J. P. Strathdee, Commando School Instructor of the Royal Marines. Since then Ross has followed the Service life, first at HMS *Seahawk*, the Royal Naval Air Station at Culdrose in Cornwall, at Deal, Kent, and now at Exmouth, Devon.

His master has the onerous but exciting duty of overseeing the last phase of commando training for recruits, including the six-mile endurance test over ravines, through water tunnels and other obstacles, and a thirty-mile march across bog-strewn countryside. For some time Ross accompanied the sergeant to the centre as a mere civilian and was left behind on training exercises, but, after a while, he was not content to be just a camp follower.

One day, as the lorry taking the squad to a starting point for the training was about to leave, Ross jumped in. That first time he just meekly followed the men, nevertheless completing the exhausting course. But from that day on, Ross has been an *ex officio* member of each 'final course', and always acts as a self-appointed advance guard. He runs on ahead, pausing once in a while to look back as if to say 'hurry along there you laggards', and the muddier and wetter he becomes the more he seems to enjoy it. He has come to know the route in detail; water, mud and heights worry him not at all. In the last three years he has completed the seven- or eight-hour trial many times and, when the men form up ready to go, Ross is the first to jump into the Service truck. As if this is not enough, Ross has also completed several nine-mile enforced marches with the recruit and young-officer classes.

He quickly becomes the firm favourite of every new squad of men, but he is treated as just one of the company and receives no privileges while the serious business is on hand. When they stop to eat, however, he noses his way from platoon to platoon seeking tit-bits, which he receives in plenty and accepts as his just reward. But he'll never get fat; the life is far too strenuous for him to increase on his seventy-pound weight.

The course completed, Ross goes home and snuggles down on his blanket, probably dreaming of the assault course and hoping that one day not an imaginary human enemy but a fat rabbit will cross his path. Combating that would naturally be all in the course of duty.

QMS Strathdee has three small children and, much as Ross loves them, he goes into a real sulk on the rare occasions he is prevented from reporting at the Royal Marine centre.

By Underground the Hard Way

Alsatians are a noble breed and, when something different in the way of an adventure befalls one of them, it is fitting that it should cause chaos on a grand scale.

The Alsatian in question became bored with being sedately exercised in Kensington Gardens – and who could blame him? One day, on the spur of the moment, he dashed off, entered Kensington High Street Underground station and carried on down to train level, where he took to the tunnel. Most probably panicking, he ran blindly through five miles of tunnels, fortunately having the good sense and the quick wit to dodge trains on the way. Railway staff and police were alerted, and there was chaos for half an hour on that section of the Underground system. Finally headed off at Gloucester Road, he turned back and was eventually cornered at Victoria station.

An astonishing episode, when it is realized that the animal could have been electrocuted at any stage along the line. Officials of the RSPCA examined him and could not find even a scratch – just sore feet. It was, they said, a miraculous escape from death.

A Greyhound Escapes

Another incident involving a dog and a railway occurred at Victoria Station, Manchester, when a greyhound in transit escaped from a baggage car. An RSPCA inspector was called and, joined by a volunteer, Mr P. Ellison, was taken to the busy heart of the station. There, underneath a narrow platform, on either side of which ran heavily-electrified main lines in constant use, the terrified dog cowered.

The rescuers were warned that a false step in either direction could be fatal, nevertheless the two men eased their way under the platform. They located the greyhound and, under extremely difficult conditions since there was not enough space for them to stand upright, made their way towards the animal, planning to gain a position on either side of the dog, thus trapping it between them. The dog, although muzzled, was understandably in a highly nervous state after twenty-four hours without food or water between two of the busiest railway lines in the North. His rescuers, however, after much patient manoeuvring managed to bring him to safety.

Strange to say, after being fed and watered, the greyhound seemed little the worse for his experience and was allowed to continue his journey.

Long Life

Nearly twenty-five years ago a stray black and white kitten was often to be seen roaming the streets of Exeter, Devon. Like most of his kind, he very soon learnt where he could get a saucer of milk and something to eat, and consequently developed regular places of call. After a while, however, he disappeared, to be seen, a week or so later, struggling in the River Exe. He was fished out exhausted but just alive. His rescuer kept him for a while, then offered him to Mrs E. D. McKie, who lived nearby, and she promptly gave him a home and a name – Toby.

Alas, poor Toby seemed fated. A few weeks afterwards he was badly bitten on the back by a rat and was rushed to the vet, who immediately performed an operation on him. Unfortunately an abscess formed, and a further operation followed. Six weeks' convalescence in the vet's care saw he was on the road to recovery and soon he developed into a fine cat. His fondness for milk (it must be Channel Island) may be a hangover from his hospital days, but it is something that has sustained him ever since. If he could speak, undoubtedly he would ascribe long life to his daily pint and raw meat, all he ever eats.

Nowadays Toby does not go out much but sleeps most of the day. On Sunday mornings, he changes his routine slightly, by making his way upstairs at the same time every week and getting on to the bed for a special half-hour's curl up.

There is something about Devon which seems to agree with cats, for the *Guinness Book of Records* states that a cat at

Clayhidon lived to the ripe old age of thirty-six, whilst another female tabby of Drewsteignton attained the age of thirty-four. By these standards Exeter's Toby is still a youngster. And it would seem that, in Devonshire, cats are not the only animals to be blessed with longevity. At Holcombe Rogus, a small village near Tiverton, lives a goose thirty years old. Long ago the family had eyes on her for a Christmas dinner, but she had a personality; she was spared and for all these years has been one of the family. So she toddles round the garden sampling any vegetables she fancies, living on to see yet another Christmas. It is not often that a ten-pound goose is kept as a pet, and it is certainly not often that a goose lives to such an old age.

Badgers Saved by Public Opinion

So often, in cases of cruelty to animals the average member of the public feels strongly but nevertheless helpless, and wishes he could do something other than sympathize. In the West Country recently public opposition forced the cancellation of a widely-publicized badger dig.

It was one of those rare occasions when public opinion could be seen to have been effective. A heartening example of what can be accomplished by a few people with knowledge and determination.

It had been arranged that twelve Cornish diggers from Tintagel and six from Somerset would take part in hunting the badgers, and it was no doubt meant to be a happy factor that the quarry would be shot and buried – not eaten. The man who was the spokesman for the 'sportsmen' stated that badgers caused a lot of damage, adding that tractors could drop into a badger's sett and endanger human life.

In a heated exchange which took place in front of television cameras, a leading West Country authority on the badger asked why the animal was being hunted and received the reply that it exercised the hunters' muscles, and the killing of badgers was a sport *and* a necessity – a strange arrangement of priorities. An *Alice in Wonderland* atmosphere crept into the arguments, when Inspector Lardner of the RSPCA said that his society was totally opposed to the needless taking of a wild animal's life, whereupon the spokesman for the hunters agreed and offered to take up a collection on behalf of the society's funds.

Lord Douglas, a member of the Cornish Naturalists' Trust, said he had been shocked to hear that a dig was to take place and considered it an exercise in sadism.

Another member said that badgers with their nocturnal habits were beneficial to the area. Their main food was earthworms, slugs and baby rabbits.

After arguments and altercations, the dig was called off and the hunters dispersed, several of them admitting they could not afford to proceed in the face of the obvious public opposition.

A Postman and His Shadow

There is always the odd one out! Most dogs seem to have a built-in dislike of postmen, for whom being bitten by dogs is an occupational hazard. Whilst there are many theories about this, no one seems able to identify exactly the reason for the animosity. It was left to Laddie, a black and white Collie cross, in the town of Alloa, Clackmannanshire, Scotland, to reverse the trend; he suddenly became an avid admirer of the postman Bob Watson, in whose 'walk' Laddie's owner lives.

The story started some four years ago when Laddie suddenly developed an interest in Bob. He began to bother his owner to let him out earlier, so that he could take up his post at the gate and when the postman arrived he would go delirious with joy, jumping up, licking and bounding about. Then he began to follow him until the round was completed. If any other dogs approached his friend, Laddie would quickly become possessive and see them off. On arrival at the sorting office, Laddie would wait patiently outside while the postman entered to start sorting letters for his second round. When Bob Watson left the office, the dog would fall in beside him and again complete the circuit. The strange thing is that Bob has an Alsatian of his own and never consciously did anything to attract his admirer.

As time went on man and dog were almost inseparable whilst on duty, and on the rare occasions when the postman was alone, he was bombarded with questions as to Laddie's whereabouts, all along his route; many people in the vicinity regularly fed the dog tit-bits.

At the end of the second delivery, when Bob returned to the sorting office, the dog always knew that it was the end of the working day and would go home. But one day he stayed, and followed his friend when he cycled home. Naturally with a dog at home this was embarrassing. Once it became a habit, Laddie would lie down outside the postman's house waiting an opportunity to get in, and the postman's Alsatian would snarl at the window trying to get out. The game of hide-and-seek eventually taxed the brain of both man and dog. Bob tried everything. He thought he had found an answer by riding his cycle into a council yard and going through to the back and home that way. Then one day, to his amazement, he found that Laddie had seen him into the front of the yard and had promptly turned about, run round the block, crossed another street, descended some steps and arrived to greet Bob as he came out at the back.

The game developed into a battle of wits. The postman would dodge down alleys and take new streets, but always Laddie seemed to anticipate his subterfuge. It reached the stage when Laddie would turn up even when Bob and his wife were out shopping on a Saturday. Shopping finished, they would arrive at the car park, and as the key was being fitted into the car door, Bob's wife would say, 'Don't look now, but I think you've got company' – and there, sure enough, was Laddie, who had obviously formed a fair idea of where to find his 'pin-up' even on off-duty periods.

A difficult situation, but what man could repudiate such love? When a relief man takes over the round for holidays, Laddie does not condescend to spare him so much as a glance. When Bob Watson retires, he intends to take Laddie for the occasional walk.

Laddie has in fact won approbation in several ways. On one of the rare occasions he was not in attendance, Bob was bitten by another dog – postman-biting is as much a canine sport in Alloa as anywhere else – and Laddie makes an efficient guard. He is indeed a welcome visitor at the sorting office – the only dog ever wanted there. The last word must come from Alloa's assistant postmaster: 'At least one of our men has to receive treatment for a dog-bite each month. If Laddie keeps this figure down, then I'm all in favour of him becoming a delivery dog.'

The World of the Horse

Horses of the Household Cavalry

Every year hundreds of thousands of people in London watch the Household Cavalry mounting guard in Whitehall. The daily ceremony, which is a magnet for overseas visitors, is viewed with an admiration equally divided between the man in his plumed helmet and shining cuirass, and the horse which is just as faultlessly turned out. The story of these magnificent horses is an interesting one and, as with so many public spectacles, a great deal goes on behind the scenes in preparation for the brief hours of glory.

Since their formation in the second half of the seventeenth century, the two regiments – the Life Guards, and the Blues and Royals – which make up the Household Cavalry have had a brilliant record in almost every war in which this country has been engaged. Now the days of skirmishing and glittering charges have gone. Every soldier is now trained in modern mechanical warfare, but fortunately two squadrons, totalling some 250 men, are retained as mounted ceremonial troops.

Almost all their animals come from the Republic of Ireland, to which a purchasing commission goes twice a year. There are several dealers, mostly in Counties Cork and Waterford, who, aware of the Army's requirements, are ever watchful for the right type of horse. The standards are high. In brief, the requirements are that the animals must average sixteen hands (a hand is four inches) in height, have a reasonably placid temperament, and be from four to five years old. All the horses are black in colour, except for the trumpeters' mounts which are always grey.

The selected horses are brought back to England to the remount depot at Melton Mowbray, and there they commence the long training to fit them for the role they will play. At brilliant royal events and other state occasions, besides on normal guard duties, these animals will display the grace and dignity for which they are famous. The training period for the horses varies between twelve and eighteen months, and the curriculum includes familiarizing them with military bands and crowds. At last, however, they are ready to take their places with the Household Cavalry, two squadrons of which are stationed in London.

As each horse joins his appointed squadron, he is given a name, and that name commences with a different letter of the alphabet each year. Thus all who joined in 1968 have a name beginning with T – Taffy, Taplow, Terrorist, Tim and Tiverton are examples. In 1969, Ulysses, Usk, Uttoxeter, etc, joined the family. Each animal has a stall with his name painted above, and he soon learns that he has entered a world offering a standard of comfort and care exceeding that offered to humans by the welfare state.

The stables are even visited daily by the regimental veterinary officer, accompanied by the farrier major, and with his rider ever watchful for the slightest upset, knock, sore or bruise, no time is lost in reporting even minor ailments. A slight sore on a horse's back leads to hasty consultations. Perhaps it can be traced to a girth webbing that has become hard with constant whitening. 'Soften it up by scrubbing or get a new one,' is the order. There are, of course, the many small disabilities which could be called the hazards of the trade. 'Speedy cut' is caused by the horse rubbing his own fetlock. 'Tread' is due to a sore foot where he has been trodden on by the horse following him. A fluffiness on the coat of an animal leads to a thorough examination, particularly if he is already on a special diet. 'Overreach' is another occupational hazard and is, to all intents and purposes, caused by a horse treading on his own heels. Once reported sick, the horse is treated and watched, and remains on the treatment book until he is cured. Carefully examined by the regimental veterinary officer and the farrier major, a horse walks or trots before them to see if his complaint or injury is being cleared. The snatches of conversation in the stable dispensary are for all the world like those at a hospital. 'What shall I give Turnabout this morning, sir? Ten of these?' holding up a bottle of pills.

Food, of course, is important. Basically, it consists of oats, bran and green fodder, but it is varied from time to time.

Rarely are there more serious troubles. Sometimes during the night a pair of horses may start kicking or biting. There was an occasion, too, when a horse took fright and ran away with his rider through the thickest of traffic at Hyde Park Corner. He only came to rest after having jumped over a taxi and spreadeagled himself among some cars. Miraculously neither horse nor rider was seriously hurt.

Those who deal with the horses agree that they are amazing animals. Physically strong, they are none the less creatures of habit and not very intelligent as animals go. If their routine is upset they have no emotional reserves to call on, and are liable to do something stupid. The men of the cavalry are of the firm opinion that domestic animals, such as the cat and the dog, and even the pig, show more general intelligence;

mules are far more intelligent. Nevertheless, it is extremely rare for a horse trained for cavalry duty to fail to live up to expectations. Only very occasionally is one found to be temperamentally unsuitable.

The trooper who will ride a particular horse and attend to his every want is a volunteer; either a fondness for horses or the search for a change from mechanical monsters will have drawn him to the mounted squadrons. Man and horse settle down to a perfect partnership. The animal is fed, watered, groomed and, when his time comes for guard duty, takes his place with eleven others for a 'short' guard or, if the Queen is in residence, a 'long' guard.

Preparation of a horse for duty takes perhaps an hour or more, for he is brushed and groomed until his coat is gleaming. Then, saddled, the guard mount and commence the stately ride down the Mall to Whitehall. The ceremony of mounting the guard completed, man and beast take up their appointed places to be gazed at, admired and photographed. The horses take to this life quite well and show no signs of impatience or boredom while they stand for an hour in full view of the public. They are then released to stand easy in the stables out of sight for another hour before their turn for duty comes round again. At the end of five hours they make their sedate way back to stables.

Of course, the life of Household Cavalry horses is not confined to guard duty. There are the special occasions when they accompany the monarch or distinguished visitors. There is also the military tattoo, when some of the horses prove to be magnificent jumpers. Once a year there is a fourteen-day camp at Pirbright, a break which must count to them as a summer holiday.

Sometimes the horses of the Household Cavalry go farther afield and, in 1969, when forty-two of them were returning from performing at the Berlin military tattoo, tragedy occurred. They embarked at Hamburg on the 8,000-ton ferry *Prinz Hamlet*. Soon after clearing the harbour, and whilst still in the restricted waters of the Elbe estuary, the ship was struck by a terrific gale which caused it to list 45°. For the next ninety minutes the thirty-three Army grooms fought to soothe the panicking animals. Ladybird, fourteen years of age, fell heavily and cut an artery; she had to be destroyed. Soon afterwards, three others, Ocean, Marina and Keystone, died from injuries and exhaustion. When the ferry eventually docked at Harwich after this gruelling voyage, the remaining horses were taken to Wellington Barracks, where many of them were treated for minor injuries. It was a terrifying experience, and had it not been for the calm efficiency and devotion of the grooms, many more animals would have been lost. It was a long time before the gloom which descended on the barracks at this tragic happening was dispersed.

If it is possible to outshine the grandeur of the ordinary Household Cavalry, it is only by their own fully mounted military band, where horses and men with glittering accoutrements and instruments make a wonderfully colourful sight. The band horses receive the same basic training as the troop horses, though perhaps the steadiest and most placid are chosen to carry musicians.

Special attention is paid to the drum horse and, since 1812, when the register shows that he was a 'pye' (pie) bald of fifteen hands, the horse holding this premier position has usually been a skewbald or piebald. These horses must be of much stronger build than the average cavalry horse and seventeen hands in height. The solid silver kettle-drums which they carry are to be seen in the Household Cavalry museum at Windsor, and very ornate and handsome they are. Apart altogether from the other accoutrements, the drums themselves weigh 118 pounds. Pride of the drum horse's apparel is the shabrack, which on ceremonial occasions serves as a saddlecloth; a red, bearded ornament hangs under his chin.

The present drum horses are Hercules and Hector. When dressed for an occasion their ears go up, their heads are held high, their step becomes youthful; each horse obviously adores the music and revels in the part he is playing. Possibly the general admiration they receive has some effect, for they always tend to become real characters. In recent years, through television, they have been seen by millions. They are always named after ancient heroes, so that there has been a Caesar, Alexander, Pompey and Hannibal. Pompey was probably the most famous of all. He was foaled in 1934 in Holland, and he died just a week after his last parade in Edinburgh in 1953, at the honourable age of nineteen. He used to appear with superb effect, particularly on Royal Tournament occasions.

It was always the practice to have the horses put down at the end of their Service life; it was believed that this was much the best thing to do, as the animals could rarely settle to being away from the routine of the troop stables, of which they had for so long been a part. Whilst this had always been the rule, many animal-lovers were shocked by it, particularly when publicity was given in November 1969 to the fact that there was always the possibility that the animals would pass from the knacker's yard to continental dinner tables. Angry protests flooded the Ministry of Defence and the Army authorities, and within a few days the RSPCA officials were exploring the position.

Results quickly followed. Money and nearly a hundred offers to save the unwanted horses poured in, one offer to have an animal coming from as far afield as Illinois in the

Amused, apprehensive, curious. The age at which everyone falls for them

Watch your step, brother – something odd here

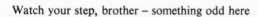

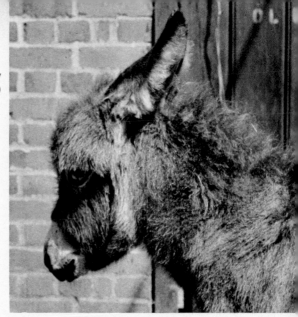

Youth at the donkey farm (*story, page 74*)

Bill, the badger with the built-in clock (*story, page 22*)

Ralph, the Alsatian who won obedience and agility trials (*story, page 30*)

Bounce, the roe deer, with his first head of antlers (*story, page 98*)

Pageantry and patience (*story, page 49*)

Police horses being schooled to jump 'bodies' (*story, page 58*)

United States. Within a few days £1,000 had poured into the fighting fund, including many contributions from pensioners. The Ministry of Defence had talks with the RSPCA, and within a short while a formula acceptable to both was agreed upon so that in future the horses will be placed in suitable homes, rather than be destroyed. It remains to be seen whether the animals can in fact readjust themselves to 'civvy' street.

So we must leave these fine animals in their stables in London, each in a stall with a name painted above. High Noon, Mirabelle, Lorelli, Quo Vadis, Kangaroo, Nelly Dean, even Trotsky and Neo Gothic are content while they are within sound of the trumpet and the care of their rider, who usually becomes enormously fond of them.

Famous in War

In spite of an apparent lack of intelligence, a horse never forgets what he has once learnt, and by the time he has served six months in a regiment he knows every trumpet call. In the days when horses played a major part in war, the steed shared all the hopes and fears of his rider. Unless the horse was hit in the skull or the heart, he always remained standing. If an unwounded horse lost his rider, he would continue to run with his companions until something threw him out of step, when he would gallop aimlessly about, neighing with fear but never leaving the field. Even in the excitement, he would avoid trampling the bodies of killed or wounded. Riderless steeds would usually fall in together for company until the trumpet call brought them all back to the ranks. Many remarkable stories have been recorded about the way the animals behaved on these wretchedly chaotic occasions. One notable horse was the charger Salamanca, belonging to Sir

John Elley, a famous soldier who rose from the ranks to became a major-general. Whenever Salamanca was involved in a mêlée on the battlefield he would kick and bite all the French horses round him, but he never made the mistake of attacking his own compatriots.

Many horses have won fame in the various campaigns for  which British troops have used them over the years. There was Freddie, for instance, of the 2nd Life Guards, who went through the whole of the South African campaign, fighting in all the major battles and travelling 1,778 miles. He was the only survivor of his troop and, in 1903, when he was the leading file at the Royal Tournament, he was noticed by Queen Alexandra. Having learnt his history, she declared he deserved a medal, and he was duly awarded the Queen's South Africa medal with six clasps, which he wore below his breastplate on special occasions. When the time came for him to be retired, he was given the freedom of Combermere Barracks, Windsor, and lived out his days roaming at will, a firm favourite with all. When he died, he was buried close to the riding school.

Another famous charger was Moifaa, and Lord Kitchener rode him in the coronation procession of Edward VII. This horse not only won the Grand National, but was also purchased by the king. A famous troop horse was Jock, who served at the Battle of Waterloo. He was a great favourite with all and, when he died, was buried in Hyde Park. Vonolel, Lord Roberts' white Arab charger, went right through the Afghan campaign and was consequently awarded the campaign medal.

When a favourite horse died, his hoof was often mounted. This originated when some officers would falsely certify a horse was dead in order to obtain the money for replacement. To stop this practice, an order was issued in 1798 that all horses' hooves were to be numbered. When an animal died, one hoof was to be removed and sent in with the request for a replacement horse. In the Household Cavalry Museum at Windsor there are several silver-mounted hooves to commemorate particularly renowned horses.

Police Horses

Not only London has mounted police. In many provincial towns a few are used, always earning admiration not only for their impeccable turn-out but for the superb training which enables them to stand firm in a jostling crowd of humans, or in the mid-stream of the roaring, coughing, smoke-emitting traffic. People who have travelled extensively often remark on the similarity of the mounted policemen in other countries. The reason is simple: many overseas policemen receive their training at the same place, Imber Court, near Hampton Court in Surrey. This establishment, founded in 1920, is run by the Metropolitan Police, but many other cities send their horses and riders to be trained there. So do a number of Commonwealth and other countries such as South Africa, Malta, Nigeria and Jordan.

There were two 'pursuit horses' attached to Bow Street Court as long ago as 1758, but it is of course only since 1920 that the mounted section of the Metropolitan Police has created the image that we now know.

Almost all their fine animals come from Yorkshire, and to be chosen a horse must pass fairly stringent tests. He must be a three-quarter bred (a light to heavy hunter), with enough breeding to give a good appearance. He must be sixteen hands in height and have good feet – essential when one remembers that most of his working life will be spent on hard roads. Age, too, must be carefully considered, for a horse continues to grow and develop until he is five. Therefore an animal from three to five years of age and unbroken is most likely to be selected, for it is much easier to train from scratch than to re-train. Over and above all these attributes the horse must have a quiet temperament if he is to withstand the exacting requirements of a public life.

When the horses arrive at Imber Court, they usually undergo a twenty-two week course of training. Part of this takes place in the riding school on a long rein, and then comes the outside schooling. This, to visitors privileged to watch, is a fascinating sight. Basically it is designed to bring the horse up against all the hazards and surprises likely to be found on the beat. It tests his courage and nerve, and teaches the super-obedience which the horse must possess.

The course comprises many hazards, commencing with the opening and closing of a gate, which gives some training in side-stepping into a crowd. There are dummies lying on small jumps, which must be unhesitatingly stepped or jumped over. A horse hates a yielding surface, so one of the obstacles is a platform of old tyres, traversed very gingerly at first but which soon is accepted. Then comes a tunnel and, quite an ordeal, an oil-drum full of stones, which is dropped from a height on to some corrugated iron just as the horse is passing. Ever up to date, the trainers now have a series of flags and banners which the animals must pass and even go under. Big drums, cymbals and other minor items create bedlam, but the horse, at one with his rider, remains quiet and calm. The training through these methods must be nerve-racking at first but it is based on an association of ideas. If the first time a horse passes a suspicious or noisy obstacle he receives a handful of corn, after a while the noise is associated with the corn that he had the first time – a pleasurable memory. Since the horse is a creature of herd instincts, it always helps to have another horse just beyond a nuisance or a difficult spot. The trainee, seeing the other horse, will make for him for companionship. It is a stock saying at Imber Court that you can teach nothing by fear.

Something in the region of twenty horses a year are taken on at the establishment and the average age of those in the force is sixteen. They often serve until they are twenty-three. It reflects great credit on all concerned that the failure rate is not more than two per cent; the same rate, incidentally, applies to the humans, all of whom are volunteers.

The Metropolitan Mounted Branch today numbers 201 horses and 210 men, and these are spread over four districts, totalling some twenty-four stations. Each man keeps the mount first allotted to him and is responsible for his grooming. Needless to say, after a while each comes to think his own horse is the best. Man and mount do a set patrol of three hours a day but sometimes, on special occasions such as big football matches, a day can be as long as eight or even ten hours. No State or near-State occasion is ever without the mounted police. Another field of duty is the patrolling of parks and open spaces which is much more easily and thoroughly accomplished by a mounted man.

The public disturbances which seem to be a feature of our time give the mounted police much extra work, yet there is no doubt that both men and horses earn considerable public esteem as a result. The Grosvenor Square demonstrations of

1969 were probably the most gruelling exercise in recent years for both man and horse – 174 mounted men took part in the mêlée and came through with flying colours. This disturbance caused many minor injuries to the horses, but there was a humorous side. One beautiful horse, Sambo, although exceptionally good in every other way, had, as a young remount, a tendency to bite. That training at Imber Court and on division had paid dividends was illustrated by his actions at Grosvenor Square. Even after a blow on the head with a stick, and although he at first gave the impression that he might retaliate, skilful handling by his rider countered any return to his former bad habit. Another horse was injured in the neck with a broken pole, and numerous weapons of a similar nature were used. Through it all the horses remained calm.

Some measure of the admiration felt for them can be gleaned from the fact that after the demonstration the police were inundated with gifts for the animals. The admiring public sent in a total of some five hundredweight of lump sugar; surely this could have only happened in Britain! A farmer in Essex sent a ton of hay, and the police were overwhelmed with offers from people ready to have injured horses for a period of convalescence.

Sorita of Southwark, Trixy of Brixton, Quebec of Hyde Park, Virgil of New Scotland Yard, Umpire of Tooting, and Banner of Rochester Row, who was a gift horse from the Queen, have all fulfilled certain basic requirements and they have all had the same training. Yet each horse has his own character, his own particular likes and dislikes, his own especial extra qualities.

Many exceptional horses have passed through Imber Court. Ethel, for instance, stationed at Brixton, is not only a superb horse for normal police work but she has been the star turn at almost all the events in the country for which police horses enter. As long ago as 1955 she won the challenge cup for the best-trained horse in the United Kingdom, and has been collecting honours ever since. Gymkhanas, horse shows and the Horse of the Year Show are other events which usefully further the training of man and mount. In all these, police entries are very successful.

Undoubtedly, the ultimate accolade for a horse is to be selected as the mount for Her Majesty the Queen at the annual Trooping of the Colour ceremony. For years Winston had the honour. A chestnut, ridden by George VI on several parades, he was a half-brother to the famous show jumper Foxhunter, and he thoroughly enjoyed the panoply of State. Unfortunately he had to be destroyed after an accident in 1957. The next to be honoured was Imperial, a chestnut gelding, who performed equally well. They all have their likes and dislikes: Imperial, for instance, loathed the very sight of a London bus.

Of them all, however, it is Royal whose memory lives on. After years of service he died in 1950. Nevertheless, for many, many years to come he will probably still be in service, for his skeleton is in the classroom at Imber Court, where it is used to teach recruits something of the anatomy of the mounted man's best friend – his horse.

In charge of Imber Court is Commander A. R. Deates, MVO.

Descendants of Knights' Chargers

When the Lord Mayor of London takes his seat for the age-old tradition of the Lord Mayor's Show, the coach is pulled by six dapple-grey Shire horses. Since 1839, it has also been the privilege of such horses to draw the coach of the Speaker of the House of Commons on ceremonial occasions. Two Shires, appropriately named Royal and Sovereign, were used in the coronation of Queen Elizabeth II.

Few sights can compare with the dignity and turn-out of these carefully matched animals at the Lord Mayor's Show. They look as if they have no other function in life but this – yet what a change such ceremony is from their normal daily round of delivering beer to the public houses within a five-mile radius of the city. Even on this mundane task, however, these horses are a grand sight, their shining, be-ribboned harness bringing a touch of colour and romance to the city streets. To older people they are a nostalgic glimpse of the past, but they also fascinate the members of the younger generation.

When Samual Whitbread the brewer purchased his first Shire horses in 1742, he set a pattern which was to continue unbroken for over 200 years. Within a few years he had thirty horses, and he purchased some farmland at Barkingside so that they could enjoy grazing and a well-earned holiday in the summer months.

The number grew and, prior to the First World War, there were well over 400 heavy horses employed by the brewery. As the mechanical age advanced, so the number of horses was reduced, until today there are but twenty-two. Happily the company does not intend to reduce the figure further.

Once an essential feature of the countryside, Shire horses are the descendants of the chargers used by medieval knights, as at the battle of Agincourt. They were bred to a size and strength which would enable them to carry the weight of their own and their rider's armour into battle without undue fatigue. The majority of the animals owned by the brewery are now bred in Cheshire, Lancashire and Yorkshire, where they receive their early training up to the age of five. They are then sent to the London stables for a further period of training to get them used to the city streets. Infinite care and patience is taken to make sure that the pairs are matched, not only in strength, pulling-power, height, weight and colour but also in temperament. Pulling-power is a dominant factor, for a loaded dray weighs approximately thirty-five hundredweight – quite something to start and stop in traffic. The six horses of the Lord Mayor's coach have a weight of some four and a half tons to pull.

Each horse is treated as an individual, for each has his foibles. Some prefer to work in a single-horse dray, others show a preference for a particular partner. Each horse weighs the best part of a ton and a set of shoes, which in the city jungle has to be renewed every three weeks, weighs some sixteen pounds. Each horse consumes three gallons of oats, three gallons of bran (both mixed with chaff), one stone of hay and one stone of carrots every day.

Following the tradition started by Samuel Whitbread, the horses are still turned out to grass once a year at one of the company's hop farms in Kent. Their shoes are removed and they go wild with delight, kicking their heels in pleasure.

The working life of a dray horse is from ten to thirteen years. By then, although his active life is far from complete, he has earned an honourable retirement from the heavy strain of working in the city's traffic tangle. Some go to farmers who use them for light work; others go to the Whitbread farms, where they are looked after during their old age.

There are few sights more attractive than a team of heavily-built horses at work, and their gradual reduction in numbers is a loss to city streets. Certainly, too, these lovely animals were a source of pride to all who worked with them. Here and there, Shire-horse teams are still to be found in the country-side. On one Cotswold farm a pair of magnificent greys,

Captain and Prince, do a fine day's work. They turn the scale between them at one and a half tons, and their shoes weigh eighteen pounds for the set of four. Though their owners run a modern mechanized farm, they say that many jobs can be done more efficiently by the horses. For one thing, they are able to get to the more inaccessible corners of the fields. In deep snow they more than come into their own and in cold weather, while engines jib at starting, the horses are anxious to be off. Farming apart, no local carnival or flower parade is complete without the massive dignity of Captain and Prince pulling the carnival queen's float.

Back to the Days of Dignity

For sixty-nine years on Easter Monday in the Inner Circle of Regent's Park, London, a crowd in holiday mood have thronged the pavements to see the London Harness Horse Parade, or a variant of it. When it started just after the turn of the century, and even as recently as twenty years ago, the crowds were less sophisticated than they are today; yet this magnificent free show never loses its charm or interest, and as the years pass an increasingly nostalgic atmosphere creeps in.

By all normal standards and the pattern of the mechanical age, the parade should have died long ago. It did suffer a severe decline between the wars; but it now bids fair to rise to new heights of popularity, attracting a crowd of thousands.

It was in 1885, those halcyon days when tradesmen delivered almost everything one wanted by smartly turned-out traps, vans or wagons, that London's cart-horse parade was conceived. The idea was to improve the general condition and treatment of London cart-horses, to encourage drivers to take a humane interest in their animals, and to stimulate the use of powerful cart-horses for heavy work on the streets. The first parade was held in 1886 and within twenty years entries had to be limited to 1,000, so great was its popularity. Altogether some 45,000 cart-horses were exhibited over the years. By 1965 entries had dwindled to twenty-six.

In 1904, another organization, the London Van Horse Parade, gained instant success with its first show. In 1914, 1,259 animals took part, but of course the numbers gradually declined. Since 1962, however, there has been a considerable revival of interest; the two societies have now amalgamated, which has resulted in more public attention for the event and a rise in the number of entries. Thousands watch a most beautiful procession of horses and vehicles, seeing the animals really come into their own again and take the stage with dignity and grace. At the 1970 parade there were 174 entries and the largest crowd for many years. Ponies from the Welsh marshes were there, from the Shetland Isles and the New Forest, magnificent bays, hackneys, Shire horses, and even that most patient and lovable of beasts, the donkey. All of them appear each year to take their part very seriously, as if conscious that this day when thousands of eyes are upon them is the time to prove that dignity does still matter, despite the ubiquitous, smelly, noisy combustion engine and the bad example set by the human race.

The very names of the beautifully turned-out horses prove fascinating. Welsh cobs taking part in 1970 varied from common or garden Rocky, Goldie, Bill or Flash Jack, to the more exotic Barfield Donna, Carmen, Stapleton Aztec or Pitchford Black Beauty. A 'mini' entry was that of Sally Grimshaw, aged seven, of Barnes, who drove a cart pulled by two 28-inch Shetland ponies, Tish and Tock. Her sister Jacqueline, aged eleven, was a passenger. A spotted stallion most appropriately bore the name of Measles, and a New Forest pony, Prince of Highview. A Welsh palomino rejoiced in the name of Golden Dolomite, and a companion, Regency. Winston, a magnificent Irish draught horse, had a strength and calm dignity that was a tribute to the man from whom he was named.

Each spick-and-span vehicle gave a glimpse of a gracious past: an American road cart, a sulky, caverlett trap, governess carts, dogcarts and flat trolleys; then came landaus, two- and four-wheeled gigs, trilby cars, an Italian carrozza, a phaeton, broughams, and an American surrey, and for good measure a show wagon and a Victorian bath-chair.

There were sections for private paired-horsed vehicles, donkeys and single heavy-horsed vehicles, each entry recalling forgotten aspects of the past. Boxer, a magnificent Shire, pulled a coal cart. Primrose and Holypark Duchess, both Shires, were the only entries off their usual beat, for they pull barges along the canals – pleasure boats, not the coal barges on which their predecessors worked so valiantly.

Perhaps the greatest applause goes each year to those truly superb pair and four-horse teams, most of which are of course entered by breweries. Among the light four-horsed teams, the Gilbeys' entry in 1970 consisted of horses appropriately named Gin, Whisky, Sherry and Brandy. York and Marquis, Champion and Royal, Rhyme and Reason, and John Bull and Big Ben were others present, each animal in its prime and weighing anything up to a ton. A magnificent sight were the two four-horsed teams in the show: four Suffolks, Boxer, Punch, Regent and Hero, and four Shires, Hengist and Horsa, Crown and Anchor.

Awards and rosettes are presented after the judging, and one gentleman ensures that every entry on parade has a bunch of juicy carrots. How St Francis of Assisi would have loved that man! This show does forcibly illustrate just how far we have advanced in the care of domestic animals since the day when the workaday horses were often worked to death. Now it is rare to see a woebegone or wretched animal at work.

Now Dogs are Tattooed

A scheme to give dogs a traceable tattoo number has been launched in London. At a cost of 50p a year, owners can have their pet tattooed with a number which will be registered. The animals will be anaesthetized while the tattooing takes place.

The registration mark will be placed on the dog's right flank only. The aim of the scheme is to cut down drastically the number of dogs which are stolen or lost and never recovered. The finder of a stray dog, or a potential buyer wanting to be sure that the dog he is buying is not stolen, can make a transfer-charge telephone call to Dogtrace, the organizers, who operate twenty-four hours a day.

Precautions have been taken to ensure that only veterinary surgeons or practitioners will carry out the registration.

Rescuers and Rescued

'Operation Faith'

We are constantly being reminded of the devotion dogs show towards the human race. Indeed, there are many examples in these pages of how they have been responsible for rescuing humans from certain death.

Sometimes, however, the boot is on the other foot and it is the animals which have the urge to go adventuring and get themselves into trouble. Rescuing one of them from a tight corner can be an expensive business. But while every human being has something of Scrooge in his make-up, almost everyone does his best when an animal is in trouble.

There was, for instance, the case of the Jack Russell terrier puppy, Faith, who with three companions was put into a drain at Shelley in the West Riding of Yorkshire in the hope that they would flush out some troublesome foxes. Three of the terriers returned, but Faith failed to reappear. Deeper and deeper she went, right under the busy A629 trunk road which runs between Huddersfield and Sheffield. Every effort was made to entice her back but she just could not make it. So she was given up for lost.

Days went by, then someone heard sounds from the pipe. There was much concern and shortly afterwards the West Riding County Council decided to mount 'Operation Faith'.

A seven-man road gang with pneumatic drills was the first to arrive. Then came an excavator, followed by a four-ton road-breaker. One-way traffic was put into operation, and the big dig proceeded. For nearly five hours the rescue squad persevered, removing at least twenty tons of rubble, until finally, at the bottom of a hole by then fifteen feet deep, the pipe in which Faith was trapped came into view. The men broke through the pipe, shone a torch, and there, thirty feet away, was the little terrier. A stone must have been dislodged behind Faith and trapped her, but now, after five days, she was safe. She seemed none the worse for her ordeal, and there was a grand reunion with her master.

Grateful thanks were showered on the road gang. Their comment was: 'We were best equipped to do the job. Anyhow it seemed the only humane thing to do.'

Cat in a Column

At Nottingham, work was halted on a big shopping development when a ginger cat became trapped inside a cast-iron column. He was neither a pedigree nor a very handsome cat, just an ordinary workaday moggie, but when the workmen saw his predicament they endeavoured to tempt him out with milk and tit-bits. Nothing would coax him forward, so they set to work and knocked down a brick wall and removed the fourteen foot high column to rescue him. The job took several hours, but the cat eventually ran off to live another day.

Beware Rabbit Holes

Then there was the case of a Border Lakeland terrier, Ruff, one well used to exploring rabbit holes, and even on occasions to getting trapped; he usually managed to extricate himself within an hour or two and arrive home tired but triumphant. Certainly at the age of ten he should have had

Could any lost dog look more miserable? A stray comes into the Dogs' Home, Battersea (*story, page 107*)

After the city jungle: dray horses wild with delight (*story, page 63*)

A neat side-step by Boots

Boots gives the *coup de grâce*
(*story, page 93*)

Shuna quite happily allows
Cronk to share her meal
(*story, page 97*)

Abbie picks up a needle and
hands it back, blunt end
first (*story, page 11*)

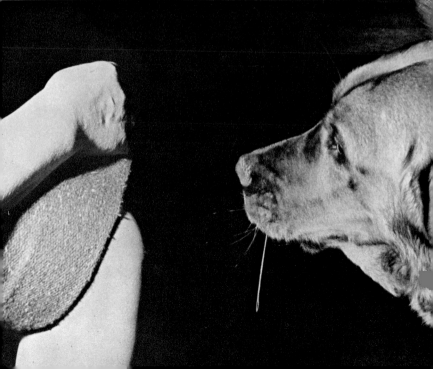

Lulu, three-year-old elephant (*story, page 104*)

more sense than to get completely stuck. Yet, one winter's day when out for a walk, he disappeared. His owners spent many hours searching for him but had to give up, hoping against hope that he would eventually return as he had always done in the past. He did, but not until six days later.

A neighbour was walking his two Golden Labradors down by the River Nidd, near Pateley Bridge in Yorkshire, when he heard a dog barking quite near. After a long search Ruff's nose was discovered sticking out of a small rabbit hole almost covered with snow on the edge of the river. Two tree roots were crossed in front of the hole and the animal was wedged in them, so that it was impossible for him to free himself. At last, however, he was pulled clear, much thinner but still full of pep. Perhaps, too, he was wiser.

Rescued by Blasting

Another lakeland terrier, a three-year-old named Sandy, became trapped behind the rock face in a disused quarry at Caldbeck, Cumberland.

Following some trail of his own, Sandy disappeared and got wedged. Fortunately his last whereabouts were known and eventually rescuers arrived, but it was no mean feat to get the dog out unharmed. Explosives, chisels and crowbars were brought into play to break through ten feet of solid rock, and finally an RSPCA inspector was able to rescue Sandy with a rope.

Although he had been trapped for forty-two hours, Sandy was as perky as ever.

Bruce, Hero of the Mudflats

A handsome nine-year-old Black Labrador with a little Alsatian in him is the hero of this story.

Four-year-old Spencer James, whose home at Monkton, Pembrokeshire, is near the river, wandered down to the water at low tide one morning with Bruce, a neighbour's dog, and became trapped in the morass of mud left by the receding water. It was not long before the boy was in difficulties, sinking until he was up to his armpits. Only his head and the top of his shoulders were clear when Bruce, with amazing understanding, quickly summed up the situation. Lying on his side, he took hold of one of the boy's shoulders to prevent him sinking farther. No one knows how long he played this heroic supporting role; it might have been ten minutes or half an hour.

Meanwhile, Spencer's mother had missed him and had searched for him in all his usual haunts. Hearing cries from the direction of the river, she hurried there, to see the boy out in the channel with Bruce holding on to his shoulder.

Spencer was rescued and his mother lost no time in getting him into a hot bath. It was then that the grateful parent found the red marks on his shoulder made by the dog's mouth – Bruce had had the intelligence not to hold on with his teeth. What is even more amazing is that he had had the initiative to lie on his side and not spreadeagle his legs, or he also would have sunk in the mud.

Bruce, who originally came from Stratford-on-Avon, is owned by Mrs G. Gard, and was given to her for company by her son, who is in the police force. From the first the dog took pleasure in the company of children living nearby and would accompany them to school. He frequently went to young Spencer's house to play with him and it was fortunate he did so on that particular day.

The dog's life-saving ability delighted but did not really surprise his owner. The neighbours were gratified when

Bruce was awarded a plaque by the RSPCA for his intelligent devotion.

Jinx Takes a Spin

During the fierce and bitter winter of 1963 a black cat strayed into the garden of a house overlooking the cove at the North Devon resort of Combe Martin. Mrs N. Laramy noticed the poor cat's terribly emaciated condition. Covered in sores, its ribs showed through its coat almost like a skeleton and it was alive with ticks.

She took the animal in, and weeks of kindness bought him back to some semblance of health, though it took much longer to make him the fine, sleek cat he is today. Thus one life of the proverbial nine, said to be the quota of every cat, had been accounted for by the time Jinx, as he came to be called, settled down with the family and became friends with Lindy, the resident spaniel.

Several years were to pass before Jinx's second life came near to forfeiture by as remarkable an experience as can fall to any cat. Perhaps because he had once been so cold, Jinx was adept at finding extra warm places in which to sit and snooze. He had several favourite hide-outs, including a cubby-hole next to a solid-fuel fire, but he was never so happy as when, wash days finished, he could crawl into the front-loading electric washing machine, fluff out his fur and sit dreaming perhaps of that hated white winter of long ago.

It was this habit which nearly cost him his second life. Wash-day was almost over, and whilst preparing a batch of woollies for the final rinse, Mrs Laramy left the front of the machine open. Unknown to her, Jinx jumped in. The woollies followed, the machine was shut and the water spin commenced. For the next four minutes the lady of the house heard a continuous strange knocking but could not trace the sound. Eventually the machine was switched off and the woollies removed. But something remained, and an exploring hand brought forth the bedraggled body of Jinx, all but lifeless. Mrs Laramy acted quickly. First she pumped the water from his stomach and then for good measure shook him upside down. Finally, as there was no sign of life, she gave him the kiss of life . . . and he twitched. Then came a gurgled meeow and finally a teaspoonful of whisky brought Jinx round. Within two hours he was eating his favourite dish, haddock, and it was not long before, sleek as ever, he was his normal self.

He still has his favourite warm spots, but now nothing will induce him to look in the direction of the whirligig. Nowadays, quite an elderly gentleman, he nestles up to the spaniel for warmth, and if the latter isn't available, the cubby-hole next to the fire will do.

A Wonderful Family

A family of 200 plus and each one known by its name: incredible but true at the Home of Rest for old and sick donkeys run by John Lockwood at Farm Cottage, Sandhills, Wormley, near Godalming in Surrey.

The behaviour of the animals now they are truly retired has to be seen to be believed. Two or three of them are blind, and should any one of these decide to set off for a walk, immediately two of those that have sight will take up station on either side of the blind one, gently edging him away from obstacles and making sure that he comes to no harm.

John Lockwood was a successful businessman but he wearied of the present-day rat race. Stalin was reported to have said that he knew his enemies and he wished he knew his friends; hearing this at a time of personal disillusionment determined John Lockwood's course of action. He sold his interests, bought the farm and decided to devote his life to unwanted donkeys. It touched his heart-strings to think that these patient beasts had given unstinted service for perhaps forty years and then, when worn out, were sold to the highest bidder to be slaughtered for their meat.

So the first donkey was purchased. He came from Ireland and was destined for the knacker's yard. The tremendous satisfaction the new owner had from his first outcast made him want to buy more. Whenever he heard of a donkey in poor health and consequently due to die, he brought it home, so that the whole scheme grew apace. For a long time now there have never been less than 170 donkeys, and sometimes the figure creeps up to 200 or more. The lengths to which John Lockwood goes for his four-footed adopted family are incredible. Rising at 4.30 A M to start the rounds, and finishing late at night, he is rarely away from the place for a whole day. On the farm it is believed that it is the humans who are daft and the donkeys who are intelligent and understand what is being done for them.

When the animals first come to him, almost all are ill. Some have no teeth, and for these food is specially boiled. Some have been badly treated, though often their owners have been merely unthinking, or at least that is John Lockwood's charitable view. The donkey, he asserts, is a delicate animal, and when depressed or sick will often just lie down and die. But not at the Farm Cottage. When a donkey arrives in a really low state, John Lockwood knows that the beast longs for some care and company, and his neighbours say he has been known to sleep in the stable with an animal until it recovers some will to live.

John Lockwood's enthusiasm is contagious. A typical

helper is Ron Hinton, baker by night and nurse to the donkeys by day, in fact in all his spare time. It is Ron who digs a grave for each donkey that dies and places a rough headboard with a name on it over the grave. People over a wide area have adopted one or more of the animals, and some make weekly calls to see them; each adoption contributes £1 to the home's running expenses, something like £200 a week. Children in the villages around also do their bit; they have discovered, for instance, that the treat of treats for the donkeys is black treacle which is thought to be good for their chests. So every week tins of treacle, sometimes amounting to gallons, are brought along. Every day is a visiting day, and it is rare that a donkey is left out; Sherry, Susie, Sandra, Popeye, Skinny, John – they all receive and answer their call.

Not only the local children visit the home, for its inmates are becoming famous. Anyone is welcome to look round at any time and old-age pensioners are as generous as any in leaving a coin in the box; in fact, few of the elderly folk go away dry-eyed. Some famous people are regular callers, for instance Ingrid Pitt, the German actress, who adopted two of the donkeys and says she would like to adopt them all.

The chief watchman of the establishment is a fine bull; he has the run of the estate at night and woe betide any intruder. When all is quiet, he takes his rest in the big stable surrounded by his less agile charges.

Donkeys are, of course, beasts of burden in a great many countries, and there are, in fact, some thirty-six different breeds in the world ranging from Spanish, Arabian and Mexican, to the Lowland. But they have much in common. Many suffer from asthma, all are susceptible to bronchitis, and the feet of almost every donkey brought in have been disgracefully neglected. Failing proper attention the animal starts to walk on his heels and the feet become deformed. By the time they reach the farm, things have often gone too far. The blacksmith comes every week but a donkey's hooves can only be rasped down a fraction each time, for the quick lies just beneath the surface. Nearly every animal at the farm has some degree of deformity in his feet.

Needless to say, there have been moments of triumph, as for instance, the old donkey which arrived in foal. Every care was taken and eventually a fine offspring was born. Seven births have now occurred and each has been successful. Then there was the case of old Hercules, a coster's donkey, who had seemingly come to the end of his useful life, and was about to be dispatched, when John Lockwood arrived. Another five minutes would have been too late, but after hard bargaining quite a big sum of money changed hands. Hercules was nursed back to sound health and today he follows his new master like a dog, whenever he can get near him.

Forty to forty-five years is the average life-span of a donkey in reasonable conditions, but many of these would have been killed off long before by being worked to death.

Any animal in real need is welcomed at the farm, for Mr Lockwood cannot say no. Naturally the other flotsam and jetsam of the animal world collect around him. Ten dogs, nine cats, five goats, ten old horses, two Shetland ponies, a goose which was the favourite pet of the late Yvonne Arnaud, the actress, and a sheep called Charlie, was the last count.

Charlie lost his mother as a newly-born lamb, so he was brought up on the bottle. On the occasions that Charlie finds himself outside the main gate of the farm instead of inside, pandemonium reigns, for many of the animal family rally round. Ten dogs of all shapes and sizes start barking, the goats, always nosy, go to investigate, the cats wake up, and there is no peace until Charlie is let in. He has a will of his own and seems to enjoy his somewhat favoured position. If he can gain access to the house, he makes for the settee, for long ago he chose this as a favourite resting place. Charlie is a master of subterfuge and the wiles that he employs to gain admittance in spite of all the precautions taken to keep him out are amusing to watch.

John Lockwood is a happy man now; he has no regrets at his strange calling and feels no envy for those who, like his brother, Sir Joseph Lockwood, chairman of EMI and other companies, occupy positions of glamour and importance, as he might well have done himself. In 1969, when the outcry about the disposal of Army horses arose, John Lockwood was one of the first to champion the cause for letting them live out their lives rather than be put down. His plea in a television interview had considerable impact.

More Donkeys

When Mr and Mrs Paul Spencer went to live near Winchcombe in the Cotswolds, they had ample ground for Mrs Spencer, who had always been fond of donkeys, to indulge her desire to keep one. So, a fine jenny was purchased and christened Snow White. She loved human company and within a few days was answering to her name. When the family went for a walk in the evening, Snow White would tag on behind the dog and the cat. This went on for the whole of one summer, but after a while it seemed unfair to deny her the company of her own kind, for she often, in the way that donkeys do, managed to convey her loneliness. In due course, therefore, another donkey christened Nancy Astor, together with her foal Benjamin Disraeli, were found for her and together the trio spent a happy winter. Snow White and her mate eventually made their own gesture of thanks by producing, as an Easter gift one year, a broken-coloured foal, called Lady Lucia.

From then on the donkey population grew. There are now a dozen or more. The Spencers assert that the animals are fascinating, highly intelligent, possessed of beautiful natures, innately curious and, above all, by their engaging habits, repay all the kindness showered upon them. Each one maintains its own individual characteristics. Nancy Astor, for instance, really does strike a pose, as if on her best behaviour at a vicarage tea party.

It is well known that a donkey is a great pacifier and that other more temperamental and difficult animals rest content when introduced to one. For instance, a donkey is often used to lead a fractious or nervous racehorse into a box, when all kinds of human persuasions have failed. Cases of a donkey harming another animal, or indeed a human, are indeed rare. The velvety softness of their mouths is unbelievable, and their feet are surprisingly delicate, as mentioned in the previous story.

This large family of donkeys, in their lovely Cotswold retreat, enjoy taking dustbaths. Groups of three or four make one of their own and the groups do not intrude upon each other. While one of a group is indulging, the others line up patiently – no pushing, no unruliness. As one finishes, so the next takes his place, to roll in ecstasy with neighs of delight.

Much thought is given to naming these animals. Usually they are watched for a while to note their idiosyncrasies, and the name evolves. There are Catherine of Aragon, Gracie Fields, Sophia Loren, Mamie Eisenhower, Silver, Valentina (born on St Valentine's Day), and last but by no means least Buzz Aldrin, foaled on the day man first set foot on the moon. At the age of three weeks Buzz became very ill and for four weeks was fed day and night with a bottle. During this time he lived on the terrace and in the garden. The house, however, was always a temptation and Buzz loved to get inside if he could, and was sometimes found stretched out on the drawing-room carpet. An avid television fan, in the evenings he would lie and watch the programmes. Climbing the stairs became one of his accomplishments and, even now, when he is no longer quite so pampered, he never loses an opportunity of popping in through the front door.

Needless to say, not much thought was wasted on a name for the brown and white jackass of the herd; he had to be Casanova!

The Baby Rabbit was a Brick

A baby rabbit recently survived an incredibly horrific adventure in the mechnical jungle of the outside world.

Concrete blocks were being made at a quarry at Axminster, Devon, and one day, as the finished product was coming off the conveyor system, the workers were amazed to see movement in one of the blocks. First a crack and then pop! the head of a tiny rabbit emerged. He struggled out by his own efforts and was sitting on top of the block before anyone could even reach him to lend a hand.

He must have been scooped up with thirty tons of sand, thrown into the weighing hopper, and then carried by conveyor to an overhead mixer, where cement and water were added and the ingredient then swirled round and round at high speed. Next he must have passed into a machine where the wet cement was hammered into blocks by pressure of 100 pounds per square inch. The blocks, which measured eighteen inches long by nine inches high by six inches thick, were then ejected on to the floor where they were to remain for drying.

True, the rabbit was in a fearfully bedraggled state, but he had survived. The men washed the cement from him, cleaned him up, dried him by an electric fire and then placed him near what must have been his point of entry. Away he hopped as if nothing had happened.

As the quarry manager said, it was a mystery how the little chap escaped unscathed, for by right he should have been suffocated, drowned, squashed or cut into pieces. What an escape story that must have been to tell his numerous brothers and sisters!

Ocean-going Goose

Walt Disney's famous little fish that swam and swam right over the dam had nothing on Lucky the goose. Where Lucky came from nobody knows and what went on in that feathered head no one can guess. Perhaps it was just a desire to see the world, perhaps even a goose falls in love; whatever the reason, he took to the water and 'he swam and he swam'. For how long is not known, but by the time the fishing trawler *Norrard Star* hove into sight twenty miles off the North Devon coast the goose was hopelessly lost and very exhausted.

Lucky summoned his last remnants of strength and swam alongside the boat where, by means of a net on the end of a pole wielded by the trawler's chief engineer, he was hoisted on to the deck. All in, but still game, Lucky tackled the food provided by the kindly crew and then, warmly settled down in the tackle locker, slept off the gruelling effects of his adventure. Obviously Lady Luck had been on his side.

Lucky was soon waddling about the deck like a trained seaman, but seven days later when the trawler was close to land near her home port, and the crew decided to put the goose into the water, Lucky seemed to have had enough swimming and steadfastly refused to leave the side of the boat. So there was nothing for it but to haul him aboard again.

When the trawler finally docked, the problem of what to do with the 'mariner' became acute. Eventually Mr Ingram, the managing director of the company owning the boat, decided to take him home to his children. Their bungalow, almost surrounded by lawn and with two fish ponds, was ideal but, as is often the case on the arrival of an unexpected visitor, some doubling-up was necessary. So the fish were all put into one pond, leaving Lucky to take possession of the other.

The bird was in surprisingly good condition, but so thin he weighed scarcely anything. At first, half a loaf a day plus some pigeon corn formed his diet. Very soon, however, he put on weight and settled for three slices of bread each day plus other tit-bits he could pick up.

Yet another surprise was in store for the rescuers, however. Everyone who professed knowledge of geese had unhesitatingly stated that Lucky was a gander. But after some weeks 'he' surprised everyone by proudly laying twelve eggs. They weighed exactly eight ounces each and were so rich that one was sufficient for a large fruit cake.

The goose has now settled down to a regular routine in her new surroundings. She swims in the pool at the same time every day and then basks in the same spot in the garden. When the master of the house arrives home, Lucky cannot get there fast enough to greet him. She flies over to him with just her toes touching the ground, and he has to stroke and make a great fuss of her before she is satisfied.

There is no question of her intelligence, nor of her inquisitive nature, for she looks inside all the flower pots, inspects the greenhouse, where her visits are disastrous for the young lettuce, and even examines the interior of the car. If the two family corgis do not stand guard over their lunch, she will have that too, and between them there is an armed neutrality, dating from the day of her arrival when she pecked one of them. She dislikes the cat, and probably fears it, for she hisses at it whenever it comes near.

After some months, Mrs Ingram felt that it was unfair to keep Lucky without company of her own kind, so a companion was obtained. It is too early yet to say how the arrangement will work, but one thing is certain, Lucky is still very much attached to her human family. And, whilst a goose is not an ideal pet to keep in a trim garden where small plants are sacrosanct, the family would not part with her.

Three Faithful Collies

The controversy over the intelligence of animals will perhaps never be resolved. There are those who are certain that animals have only instinct; others are convinced of their capacity for reasoning. Whatever the answer, animals often leave us amazed at their behaviour in difficult or dangerous circumstances.

One such example must surely be that of the three sheep-dogs belonging to a shepherd living near Callendar in the Trossachs district of Scotland. The shepherd left the farm, accompanied by his three dogs, at 9 AM on a winter's morning to see to the 1,200 sheep in his care, some of which were missing beyond the great hills which form a backcloth to the little town. But the weather deteriorated badly and he failed to return. He had been missing eleven hours when the alarm was raised by the arrival back at the farm of one of his collies. The twin hazards of heavy snowfall and thick fog made it impossible to start a search that night, but next morning an RAF mountain-rescue team, police, foresters, shepherds, gamekeepers and other volunteers, aided by a helicopter, mounted a search.

The weather was still atrocious and the helicopter had to be withdrawn, but those on foot struggled on. Eventually one of the police constables, making slow progress through the snow and mist, was halted by a deep growl. He found the two collies standing guard over the body of their master. All night they had waited in those awful conditions, and now they were ready to attack the constable as he approached. It appeared that soft snow on the hills had yielded beneath the shepherd's weight and he had fallen 500 feet to his death. The people of the Trossachs mourned the loss of one whom they had held in great affection and esteem.

One wonders what sort of reasoning went on in the minds of those dogs. Humans in the same situation would have considered which of them could best make the return journey and raise the alarm. Perhaps they would have tossed a coin for it. In the same way, two of the animals elected to stay on guard, while the other went for help.

Mongrel Saves Young Master

It was a bitter November day when Willie Fraser, aged seven, and his friend Tony went for a walk on the moorland near their home at Burnley, Lancashire. They were accompanied by Willie's constant companion, Lady, a mongrel dog who had recently attached herself to him. Probably they never intended to go far, but being boys they just wandered on. They were thinly clad; Willie wore only a jumper, vest, short trousers and rubber boots.

They started out in reasonable weather but, as often happens on the moors, conditions deteriorated rapidly. A gale-force wind blew up, bringing with it freezing sleet and heavy downpours of rain. In such conditions the two boys became hopelessly lost, and as darkness began to fall Willie could go no farther. They had been wandering for four hours and he sank down exhausted against a moorland wall. His friend stumbled off to try and get help, whilst Lady remained with her young master.

Eventually Tony was found wandering near a farmstead where the farmer's wife took him in, gleaned some of his story and immediately raised the alarm. By then it was dark, but twenty policemen accompanied by two dogs moved into the area and began what they must have felt was a pretty hopeless task. The conditions were appalling, with the rough ground becoming a thick oozy mud. Suddenly Sabre, one of the police dogs, picked up a scent which led them to Willie, half a mile away. He was still lying against the same wall but was unconscious, and over him, protecting him with her warm body, was Lady. They were some six miles from home!

The boy was rushed to hospital, where the doctor found that Willie's heart had stopped beating. They massaged it externally for half an hour and then gave the kiss of life. The heart began to beat again. The last word must come from Willie. 'It was very cold,' he said – surely the understatement of the year – 'but Lady snuggled over me to keep me warm, and I don't remember anything after that.'

Lady, in her attachment to Willie, has developed one endearing trait. Whenever Willie cries, she bounds to him and licks his face until he stops.

A Puppy's 'Thank You'

When fourteen-year-old John Foley of London lit a gas fire in his home one day, a blaze started which quickly enveloped the house. He dashed downstairs to raise the alarm and then remembered that Rex, his very small mongrel puppy, was still upstairs. Back he ran, only to be met by a wall of flame. He hesitated and then heard the dog yelping. So, getting down on to his hands and knees, John crawled up the stairs and into the room, grabbed the puppy and, hugging him close, crawled back and struggled down the stairs again. Both then ran for their lives.

The embarrassing part of it all is that Rex seems to know just what has been done for him, and his continued licking of John's face is becoming too much like washing to please a boy!

Bloodhound's Victory Roll

No collection of 'rescuers and rescued' stories would be complete without some reference to the bloodhound Capella Podlea, owned by Dr and Mrs Hull, of Coleman's Hatch, Sussex. On at least two occasions 'Dumpy', as she is affectionately known, has been successful in tracing another missing dog.

The first was in 1968 when she tracked a Sealyham terrier to a badger's sett. Capella literally ran the terrier to earth some five feet underground. When she came to the hole, she put her ear to it, listening, it seemed, for the sound of breathing. Then, satisfied, she did what was tantamount to a victory roll, by rolling over on her back as is the way with bloodhounds when they run their quarry to earth. It took several men some hours to get the terrier out, but finally he was rescued none the worse for his adventure.

The next time Capella was called upon was in 1969, when Rajah, a long-haired Chihuahua, the pet of fourteen-year-old Christopher Fulford-Brown of Sussex, disappeared through the hedge of his garden. Many hours were spent searching for him, but in vain. As a last resort, someone suggested seeking the services of the bloodhound which had been in the news, and in due course Capella was brought to the scene. Her owners felt that, after such a long period, the scent might be too faint; nevertheless, she was taken to Rajah's bed where she sniffed to pick up the scent. Then the party set off – and what a trail it proved to be. Capella led them on a twelve-mile trek across fields, through woods, under barbed wire and over boggy land. Overcoming her instinctive terror of traffic, she took her posse across four main roads, till at last, after nearly three and a half hours, the Chihuahua was found. People had seen the little dog running wildly around and had, in fact, telephoned the police, but they had mistakenly described him as a Yorkshire terrier.

So this magnificent tracker earned her second RSPCA plaque, for services very well rendered. She is the only dog ever to win this highest award twice.

Capella is descended from a bitch in the Lake District, where bloodhounds are frequently used to track humans. The Scottish police also use them, though other police forces in the United Kingdom generally choose Alsatians. Bloodhounds were extremely popular in Britain before the war, but their numbers were drastically reduced – down to five – due to the difficulty of feeding them under wartime conditions. It is estimated that there are now 900 to 1,000 in the British Isles. They have big appetites and Capella has some three pounds of meat every day in addition to biscuits and milk. Now four years old, she weighs some ninety pounds.

Peggy Gave the Alarm

Peggy, a three-year-old white and tan mongrel terrier, was given to Mr and Mrs Warren, of Torworth Road, Boreham

Wood, Hertfordshire, by an anti-vivisection society. The couple, who are in their sixties, are both incapacitated. When they retired to bed late one night, they accidentally left a candle alight. In due course it melted its plastic container and set the dressing-table and cloth smouldering. Peggy, who always sleeps in their room, was roused and went into action. From paw marks found afterwards, she had apparently first tried unsuccessfully to awaken Mr Warren. Then she had turned her attentions to his wife and, by frantically licking her hand, managed to waken her. Mrs Warren found the room full of dense smoke and quickly woke her husband. Together they managed to get out of the bedroom and the fire brigade was called. They were taken to hospital but fortunately were only detained a day or two. Two lives might well have been lost, but for a sprightly little mongrel.

A Grateful Mascot

The British serviceman has two loves, children and animals, and the number of pets, dogs in particular, that he has rescued from bad conditions whilst serving overseas and brought back to this country is huge. In the East, where mongrels are ill-treated, they are often adopted by servicemen and become great favourites. Sometimes the animals repay the kindness they have received, as in the case of Oscar, a black mongrel.

It all began when Royal Marine Commandos stationed at Dhala on the Yemen frontier prevented Oscar from being beaten by an Arab and adopted him. He was made much of, was brought back to fine condition and, of course, became inseparable from his new companions. In return, he was instrumental in preventing a surprise night attack by alerting the guards with his barking.

The time came for the 45 Commando Royal Marines to return to England and, although no one wanted to part with Oscar, the servicemen could not pay his fare. Well-wishers in England, however, hearing of their predicament, promptly raised the money for his passage. So Oscar came home with his Royal Marine friends and, after spending six months in quarantine, took part in a grand reunion.

Now Oscar is the mascot of 45 Commando Royal Marines, and is on the strength of Stonehouse Barracks, Plymouth. When the Queen visited the barracks in 1969, Oscar was on parade, and was honoured by a friendly pat from Her Majesty and by the interest of Prince Philip.

Across the Arctic

In 1969, the British Overland Arctic Expedition led by Wally Herbert arrived at Spitzbergen, after completing the first-ever overland crossing of the Arctic. It had been a fantastic journey of 478 days, 'across the roof of the world', and has since been described as one of the most gruelling feats of human endurance every undertaken.

As the expedition neared Spitzbergen, it encountered dangerous ice conditions which necessitated an air lift of men, dogs and equipment from the melting ice to HMS *Endurance*, which was standing by to return the members of the expedition to the United Kingdom. But difficulty arose over what to do with the thirty huskies which had served the humans so faithfully. Certain commercial interests at Spitzbergen arranged to rehabilitate fifteen of them, and the committee of the expedition sought the assistance of the International Society for the Protection of Animals, to see if some use could be found for the others, the only alternative being to have them put down.

The Norwegian branch of the society was contacted, with the happy outcome that, provided the ISPA could put up £1,500 – the cost of the quarantine – the dogs would be welcomed by the Norwegian Sled Dog Ambulance Club for use in the sled teams that from time to time go to the assistance of injured skiers and mountaineers. It was considered that, if the dogs were placed in that service, they would remain in their natural environment and continue to be usefully employed. At the same time, the dogs would receive a high standard of care and attention. Quarantine was necessary because mammals such as Arctic foxes and polar bears can transmit rabies, and there was no certainty that the huskies had not been in contact with such animals; polar bears had more than once entered the expedition's camp.

ISPA Husky Dog Appeal Fund was launched with the cooperation of the committee of the expedition. It is a happy thought that the necessary money was raised in the United Kingdom, and that the dogs are now working cheerfully on their missions of rescue.

It Cost Thousands – but the Fledgelings Lived

A hobby bird of the falcon family, very uncommon and only a summer visitor to Britain. Plumage dark-slate above and white, tinged with chestnut, streaked with black underneath. In flight it glides, hovering less than the kestrel.

Haunt, chiefly woods. Nest, old nest of the crow or similar bird which builds in a tree. Food, small birds and insects – the latter are caught with feet and transferred to bill. Notes, a chattering double note call.

This is the sort of information interested people unearthed in books when a pair of hobbies hit the news headlines in 1969. These birds of prey, rare visitors to Britain, were accorded VIP treatment when no less a project than a £2,000,000 pipeline was halted to enable them to launch their precious offspring into the world. The work of laying the Esso Petroleum Company's pipeline was forging forward ahead of schedule, when it was reported that the hobbies' nest with its fledgelings was directly in the line of operations at Longcross, Surrey.

The birds were actually being filmed when it was noticed that the parents, apparently disturbed by the noise of the equipment, had abandoned their young which were almost ready to fly. Representations were immediately made to the Esso Company by interested parties, including the Royal Society for the Protection of Birds, and the contractors hastily finished some welding and then ceased work and erected a protecting wire fence around the tree on which the nest was situated.

The parents immediately returned to the fledgelings, who by this time were extremely weak; but in two days they had recovered sufficiently to fly away. The halt in the operations undoubtedly saved the birds from dying and, as the species is almost extinct in Britain, it was a splendid gesture which must have cost many thousands of pounds.

Just a Humble Pigeon, But . . .

In London's Leicester Square one day in the spring of 1970 a passer-by spotted a distressed party; he telephoned the RSPCA, and immediately the full weight of the resources of the capital's rescue services went into action – for a pigeon. The bird had apparently become trapped high up in a tree, its leg being entangled in a piece of cord, and for two hours it made futile efforts to free itself.

The RSPCA alerted the fire brigade and five firemen were soon on the spot. Being unable to get their ladder into a point of vantage within the Leicester Square Gardens they called for more help and soon a forty-five foot extending ladder from Southwark was speeding to the incident. The appliance was manoeuvred into position, and temporary Sub-officer David Holland ascended, armed with a net and a knife attached to a pole. Holding the net below the bird, he severed the cord which was trapping the bird, and the pigeon dropped safely into the net. Cheers and clapping from the curious and sympathetic crowd that had inevitably collected greeted the rescue, and these were renewed when the fireman descended the ladder and concluded an eighty-minute rescue operation.

Miss Jean Gilbert of the RSPCA clinic to which the pigeon was taken reported 'nothing broken'; its rescuer could not have been showered with more congratulations had he rescued one of the crowd themselves. It remained for a German visitor who had witnessed the incident to sum it all up: 'This – you could only see it in Britain'.

Mouse Did Not Like the Programme

Leeds Radio was put off the air for thirty minutes. The cause? A mouse crossed two contact joints.

Animal Friendships

Animal friendships can be strange. There was the case of the leopard whose constant companion was a dog. From the best of motives people complained that one day the leopard would turn on the dog and kill it, so that, eventually, in deference to public concern, the two were separated. The dog died within three weeks, with nothing apparently ailing it except anguish at being parted from its friend.

Then there is the case of George the seagull, the constant companion of Clarence and Clariss, a pair of malibu storks at Chessington Zoo. George keeps a strict eye on his unusual friends and fiercely wards off any intruders. He must be possessed of a personality all his own, for he has been adopted by Britain's 25,000 Cubs.

Some of the stories which follow deal with other such oddly-assorted relationships; some tell of friendships between animals of the same species. All show the warmth of feeling that animals can have for each other.

A Tale of Two Cats

Tiger Tim, a magnificent young cat, was ginger and white and lived one side of the road. Boots, a handsome patriarchal cat, was black and white – his paws were startling white, hence his name – and he lived on the other side of the road. The two were on nodding terms as neighbours but when either of their owners went away the cats became lodgers in each other's houses.

Tiger Tim, as became his age, was playful. Boots, on the other hand, was dignified and would usually pass by majestically when the younger cat took a swipe at him with his paw. Periodically he would enter the contest, but even then no fur would ever fly. It would not be a serious confrontation but, like boxers sparring in the ring, would take place with an entire absence of spite and venom.

Such occasions remind us that felines have their own very real personalities. When the sparring commenced Boots would immediately take up a vantage point on a chair, and Tiger would attack, the bout going on for perhaps ten minutes. Boots would disdainfully wave a paw, with a look on his face which plainly said: 'I am the king of the castle and I intend to remain so without undue effort.' Finally, after repeated sorties, Tiger Tim would spring and obtain a foothold on the chair, and Boots, calmly omnipotent, would place a giant paw on his head and by sheer weight push him down. Thus the contest ended until next time.

Neither animal would ever steal or muscle in on the other's food. Tiger, in fact, never attempted to touch anything left within reach; but Boots was otherwise an incorrigible thief – nothing was sacred, not even the Sunday joint, and never did his eyes prove bigger than his massive stomach.

On one occasion Tiger's strange behaviour astonished all who saw it. From a window in the house he was observed jumping up and down on the grass with his four feet spread-eagled. Up and down like a yo-yo he went, eyes blazing and whiskers quivering. Closer inspection revealed an adder on the lawn, its writhings and turnings beating time as it were to Tiger's jumps. On the touch-line in magnificent isolation was Boots, watching every move. After a while the snake was decapitated with a spade. Its writhings continued but Tiger, just as if he knew that all was safe, ceased his sparring. Boots, now frankly bored, moved off. Never having seen a snake before, how did Tiger know he had met a dangerous foe, for there was no mistaking his demeanour.

One day a third, very elderly cat joined them. He belonged to a poor old lady, and had been her constant and only companion. Until a good home had been found for him, she had refused to be moved to hospital and, judging by his good condition, he seemed to have had more than his fair share of the available food. Poor old Micky was content to lie sleeping all day, but any sudden movement would terrify him. It was quite a time before it was realized that this was probably due to the fact that he had never been used to anyone moving quickly – his aged and crippled mistress had for years perforce moved very slowly.

When Micky first arrived, Tiger and Boots duly inspected him. After that, the two younger cats were never again seen to approach the new visitor. They seemed to size up the situation at once and to mutually agree that here was one to whom they must be charitable, that Micky was old and tired and that they should let him sleep peacefully.

Sad to say, Micky's mistress died a few weeks later and, not long afterwards, as if in sympathy, he followed her.

Big Sister Susie

High up on the Greenhow moors, Yorkshire, are the Stump Cross Caverns, a wonderland of nature whose evolution began 200,000,000 million years ago. The caves, which are open to the public, are in a very isolated position and the cabin at the entrance used to be a regular target for petty thieves and vandals. The place was not an acceptable insurance risk and the proprietor, Mrs Barbara Hanley, decided that she would obtain a guard dog to protect it. So Susie, a fine five-year-old Alsatian, became custodian of the hut at night. For a time all went well. She scared off trespassers on many occasions but eventually some intruders, obviously not on their first visit, overcame her by bursting open the door and throwing battery acid in her eyes. Not content with this, they then belaboured the poor animal with sticks and, undoubtedly pleased with themselves, made off with their paltry haul.

Well known in the district for her love of animals and for her kind heart, Mrs Hanley decided to accept her losses, which continued to occur, rather than leave her dog to take such consequences. So Susie was taken home at night and, although it took time, gradually recovered her equanimity.

At a nearby farm Jess, a black and white collie, had been found useless for working with the sheep and had spent three years chained up as a 'bark dog' to warn of the approach of strangers. The farmer, hearing of Susie's misfortune and her mistress' troubles with thieves, presented Jess to Mrs Hanley.

No one can tell what goes on in an animal's mind, but perhaps there can be genuine fellow-feeling. Certainly the Alsatian assumed the role of protector to the collie and thus began for Jess what we humans call 'rehabilitation'. Jess was petrified of anything or anybody until, by a lucky thought, she was tied up close to Susie. It took a long, long time, but gradually the confidence of the smaller dog was restored. She ceased to cringe at the approach of a human and, while Susie was about, actually became quite bold. The two animals became inseparable, surely a vivid illustration of the strong looking after the weak in the animal world.

They Live and Let Live

By and large, animals will live and let live, and only kill when they want to eat. An illustration of this and how well animals or birds usually considered inevitable enemies in the wild state can get on together, is provided by Mr Don MacCastill, a forester of Argyllshire. He has had kestrel, tawny owl, buzzard and hen harrier side by side on the same perch with no animosity or fuss between them. Many animals and birds have come into Mr MacCastill's care. Generally they have been abandoned by the parent or been injured, and whenever possible he brings them back to health and then releases them.

Among his charges have been all sorts of characters, but perhaps outstanding for general mischievousness was Cronk, the raven. Rescued when she fell out of a nest as a young bird, she quickly forged a special place for herself in the homestead. Teasing the cats unmercifully, stealing clothes pegs and even garments from the line (which could sometimes prove embarrassing) were some of her favourite pranks. Cronk would also delight in going for walks with the forester and his Labrador Shuna.

Sometimes flying, sometimes hopping sideways in step with Mr MacCastill, and often just riding in style perched on Shuna's back, her beady eyes would never miss a chance to play up something or somebody. If Rufus, the dog fox, was resting comfortably in his enclosure with his tail against the wire, Cronk would never miss the opportunity of pulling his brush through the holes. She would play with Shuna, swooping and diving over the Labrador's head, but after the one occasion that she did this to the fox, they were never allowed together again, for Rufus, quick as lightning, caught her by the neck and gave her a good shaking. Cronk had for once met her match and was petrified, but fortunately the fox had had the sense not to use the full force of his jaws as he undoubtedly would have done in the wild. Cronk took a little while to recover her equilibrium, but after a few days was pulling Rufus' brush through the wire again.

When the forester and his family recently moved to another part of the country, Cronk decided to go back to the wilds, and off she went – to be much missed by the family, and probably Rufus, too.

Rufus was orphaned when a cub and has been in captivity ever since. Now three years old, he can never be released because he would be at a loss among his wild brethren – his natural hunting instincts are limited to killing rats and mice. After a while Mr MacCastill secured a mate for him, and three gorgeous cubs were the result. If he can get into the house he is happy, and finds Shuna a great companion, though he is inclined rather to dominate her.

Mr MacCastill confesses to having a favourite species – the roe deer. He has succeeded in rearing four, but has found that the bucks should never be kept longer than a year or they become really dangerous, particularly during the rutting season, June–July, when they will attack without fear or favour. One such was Bounce, a magnificent creature, who in his second year produced a full head of ten antlers. He eventually became such a 'bad hat' that he was shipped down to Cannock Chase but, sad to say, after a while he had to be shot.

Tortoise Joins the Space Race

Animals, it seems, creep into every possible phase of our lives, not only into our domestic round but into public events. The *Daily Mail* Transatlantic Air Race of 1969 provided an example.

The first to steal some of the limelight was a strapping young colt, the offspring of Arctic Rose owned by Mr Neville Samuelson, who was to compete in the race. Arctic Rose had been due to foal a fortnight before Mr Samuelson's dash to America, but day succeeded day until it seemed impossible that the colt could be born in time. Then, early in the morning of the very day of departure, the new youngster appeared. His owner was able to roar away in his vintage Spitfire, content in the knowledge that the colt and mother were doing well. A national competition to name the colt was subsequently launched and, as a result, he was appropriately christened Air Baby.

But it was George the tortoise who stole the show, for he actually completed the course, travelling to New York and back in twenty-two hours. George was the friend of one of the competitors in the air race who, remembering the fable about the tortoise in a race, felt such a mascot was bound to bring him luck. So he smuggled George through the customs in his helmet and off they went.

In the course of their travels they slipped past more customs, were involved in a motor-bike crash and as a result spent $41 at a New York hospital, drank beer at the Fourteenth Police Precinct (his owner did, George himself had a salad), and then sped through the city at around 100 mph on the back of a speed cop's motor-cycle with its siren screaming. They eventually clocked in safely at the Post Office tower in London.

Quite an adventure for a 'hardback', apart altogether from the fact that, of the 348 competitors, George was the only tortoise.

Cygnet Makes a Friend

A cygnet, a mere two days old, was seen to fall off her mother's back; only the timely intervention of some holiday-makers saved her from an attack by two adult swans.

The tiny thing, a handful of grey fluff, more like a powder-puff than a bird, was just alive when taken to a bird sanctuary at Exmouth, Devon. Mrs B. M. Marsault, who cares for a variety of birds, took her in, but at first nothing could interest the cygnet in food. Chopped grass, insects, ant eggs, eggs, chickweed, biscuit crumbs – everything was tried in vain. Experienced in the ways of caring for birds and animals, Mrs Marsault noticed that the bird had pecked at her apron. As a last resort, she spread some food on the apron and soon the cygnet was pecking away, realizing even at that early age that there was more food in the saucer. From then on there was no more difficulty.

What more natural then that she should be christened Pavlova! With her boot-button eyes and patent-leather beak, the little bird quickly settled down and, like Topsy, growed and growed and put on weight at the rate of an ounce a day. Instead of the wide open spaces, her aquatic outings were confined to the sink, but she thrived.

One of the family at the bird home is Pasha, a handsome seven-year-old Alsatian and, from the first, he was fascinated by Pavlova. Quite early on, the cygnet, with typical feminine audacity, would sit between the dog's massive paws. Pasha was undisturbed until she gave her high-pitched squeak, but soon even this ceased to worry him. Obviously the cygnet had decided to adopt Pasha as her family, for she was still very young when she first began to preen the Alsatian.

Pavlova is now big and strong. She gets airborne from time to time, but always returns, much to the evident pleasure of Pasha. It was hoped that a home would be found in a wild-fowl community, but hand-reared birds apparently are not popular, so she remains with her adopted family. She has a pond of her own now and proudly and regally floats across its surface, while Pasha admires her from the edge.

Tiger Cubs on Holiday

Holidays at the seaside are usually considered the prerogative of humans. It is certainly not usual for a pair of tiger cubs to be included in a family party arriving at their chosen holiday resort.

Two tiger cubs born at Chessington Zoo were abandoned by their mother when they were only three weeks old. The zoo superintendent, Mr Eddy Orbell, took them home so that his family could lend a hand in giving them the constant attention they needed at that tender age, for they had to be fed every four hours day and night. All went well until the Orbells were due to go on their annual holiday to Bridport in Dorset, where they had a caravan. The various members of the family were worried about what would happen to the cubs in their absence, and unanimously decided that they must go too. Kalahanui and Karond were six weeks old at the time and weighed some ten pounds. Their daily walk on the beach became an event which delighted holidaymakers and animals alike.

But the cubs are now growing up apace and it is unlikely that they will ever again find themselves on holiday at the seaside.

Squirrel Waifs

When twelve-year-old Robert Whitehouse, of Chelwood Gate, Sussex, found a baby squirrel in the course of a nature walk, he could not believe the tiny thing was alive. Only about a week old, his eyes were not even open and there was no sign of his mother. Nutty, as he was immediately christened, was taken home and the family pooled ideas and resources in trying to keep him alive. Robert made a box into a nest and placed it behind the boiler; while his sister Barbara, aged six, produced a doll's feeding-bottle just $1\frac{3}{4}$ inches long. This they filled with a mixture of warm water, milk and glucose and fed the squirrel regularly.

Nutty, who weighed only three ounces, responded well and within a few days began to thrive. After ten days his diet was enlarged, until he was having custard, chocolate, biscuits and, above all, shelled nuts. Every new food was eagerly tried.

In a matter of weeks, Nutty was substituting the members of the family for trees, and would jump from one to another, hiding nuts in their pockets. When all his energy was expended, he would sit on someone's shoulder purring – and it was a purr like a kitten's. He soon began to invent his own games. If his tail was tweaked, he would immediately retaliate by pulling the nearest person's hair. But one thing that amazed them all was that though his claws soon became wicked-looking and though he could not retract them as a cat can, he only made the slightest scratches and never harmed even a pair of stockings.

Nutty soon grew to a fine size and weighed twelve and a half ounces. When the weather improved the family decided to set him free to join the squirrels in the nearby oak trees. He was often seen afterwards, but he would never come to hand.

A few days after Nutty had been released, some school friends of the Whitehouses brought another abandoned squirrel to them – this time an albino (a white one), a rare thing in the world of squirrels. Quite possibly this one had been discarded by his parents, as so often happens in nature when a member of the family does not conform to the usual standards. The poor little chap was covered in mud and vermin, but with the experience gained from Nutty he was easier to establish. He, too, was fed on milk to start with, but whilst he soon began to clamber about, he was not nearly so tame as his predecessor.

One day he disappeared and was missing for twenty-four hours, but eventually he came racing along the road with the family cat, Puss, in hot pursuit. Nutty II made it, however, and showed unmistakable signs of being glad to be home again. In fact, the cat plays happily with the squirrel, and possibly the chase home was not due to the hunting instinct, but was the performance of a self-appointed task, getting the truant back home.

As Nutty II grew bigger there was some concern about keeping him in confined quarters, so a wire enclosure was built round a tree to give him as much natural free movement as possible. This he certainly seems to appreciate. He cannot be released as was the first Nutty, for it is doubtful if an albino would ever be accepted by other squirrels. So a pet he will remain.

The Elephant and the Mouse

There are few animals more intelligent than the elephant; the species, when young, is particularly appealing. Lulu, who came by 'air mail' from Thailand to delight all who visit Chessington Zoo, is no exception. On her arrival, she was taken to her centrally-heated quarters and within a few days a remarkable friendship was born. A mouse, perhaps attracted by the warmth of the elephant house, took up residence and he and Lulu have been almost inseparable ever since. With crumbs from the big fellow's table an added attraction, he runs up and down Lulu's trunk with careless abandon, and his favourite seat of vantage is high up at the base of the trunk near the forehead, where he sits and watches the world go by.

When Lulu settled down, she developed a gargantuan appetite and her daily menu at the age of two was seventy-five bread rolls, twelve currant buns, twelve pints of milk, some apples and quantities of hay. In addition, she needed two buckets of water, carefully warmed so as not to cause wind or indigestion. Now that she is growing up (she now stands thirty-eight inches high), her diet includes more varied solids – bananas, bran, oats and hay – but she has never forgotten her first meal in England, bread and milk, which she had at two-hourly intervals; it is still her favourite dish.

Lulu, a delightfully friendly animal, and apparently without fear, spends much time each day swaying to and fro. This is called weaving, and it is believed that by so doing she comforts herself.

When she is fully grown she will weigh anything from three to four tons, and she will probably attain an age of fifty to sixty years. One thing is certain, she will outlive by many,

many years that bosom friend of hers, who has made non-sense of the legend that the sight of a mouse sends an elephant into a frenzy of fear.

A Dog and His Bone

It is well known that soldiers have an amazing fondness for animals of all types. As long ago as 1904, the 2nd Life Guards had a regimental bear and when the regiment entrained at King's Cross on one occasion, he escaped. He was followed by a crowd of some 1,000 people, and a report of those days says that he was regrettably beaten by a few bystanders. Finally, he was 'arrested' by the police and kept in their protection until the regiment claimed him. There was a mongrel dog which followed the Royal Horse Guards throughout the Peninsular campaign, and another was given a silver collar with the names of the battles at which he had been present in South Africa inscribed upon it. Another instance of animal friendship occurs frequently in stables, where a cat or a dog will became inseparable from a certain horse. One mongrel dog, called Boots, always kept close to Hannibal, former drumhorse of the Blues, and shared his loose box. On one occasion Boots really made his mark.

It happened at one of the ever-popular military tournaments where, walking round one evening before the show began, Boots wandered into the area where the naval teams were rehearsing their gun-carriage contest. Among these was one West Country team which had been dogged by ill luck and for which nothing seemed to be going right. For some time Boots watched their efforts with disdain and then, as if to show it, he strolled over to the gun carriage and cocked his leg. One can well imagine the comments that must have come from the members of the gun team. That night, however, the team won, and after that the dog was in high favour, for had he not brought them luck?

From then on he was given the freedom of the naval kitchens and, of course, all the best bones. The sequel was not so amusing. A few days later Hannibal was found to have a large weal on his flank. The trooper in charge got into hot water for alleged carelessness, and it was only when the stables were cleared out that the truth of the matter became evident. Boots had been given a large shin-bone by his sailor friends and, in the way that dogs do, had buried it in the straw of Hannibal's loose box. The horse had lain on it all night – thus the weal. Boots, however, still soldiers on. He is hale and hearty and belongs to an ex-corporal major, who now lives in Windsor.

Migration by Jet

An American robin hatched so late that it had not learned to fly in time to join the annual migration of its fellows from Detroit to Miami, Florida.

One of the pilots of Eastern Airlines, however, had a soft heart and a brainwave. He placed the robin in a cage, and the cage on a vacant seat of his jet passenger plane.

Certainly the robin did his tour on the grand scale, but the kind-hearted pilot is wondering whether he has not started something, and whether the robin will in due course expect the return trip with, of course, all his relations.

Dog turns Vegetarian

A half-breed poodle, owned by Lord and Lady Dowding, has followed of his own accord the example set by his owners. He has become a vegetarian. His meals consist of nut or cheese dishes, raw carrots, nuts, egg yolks and biscuits.

The Battersea Dogs' Home

As he hears a different step, the little black and tan mongrel perks up. Rising on his hind legs, his front paws scratching at the bars, tail wagging furiously, he sniffs frantically with anticipation and hope. Can it possibly be someone coming for him? In seconds it is all over, he slinks back to curl up miserably as he has done a hundred times before – a picture of utter dejection. This isn't his master or mistress; once again he must give up hope. This is something that happens every day to most of the animals in the greatest dogs' home in the world – at Battersea, London.

Every week anything between 200 and 400 dogs are collected from police stations all over London, where they have been taken as strays. Some are in fine fettle and are obviously genuinely lost. Most were once eagerly-adopted pets. Some have been attached to the same family for years; others were purchased with great enthusiasm but, after a few days or weeks, when the novelty had worn off, were discarded as a nuisance. In the holiday season particularly, a large number are deliberately 'lost', so that their owners do not have to take them with them or pay to have them boarded.

The mind of a dog-lover boggles at the mentality of a human who can have a dog for years and then, when it grows 'too large', becomes old or dirty, or is about to have pups, can take it to some deserted spot and make off, leaving it well behind.

But these are the less tragic cases which occur every day at the Home. Some of the dogs are really ill when they are brought in and have to be destroyed. This, too, is the fate of most of the puppies under six months, which have not been inoculated against distemper and hard-pad. Every week five ambulances tour the Greater London area calling at 189 police stations. Almost every station will have one or more strays waiting. Some will be starving, though if they have been at a police station for even a few hours, the edge will have been taken off their appetite by the kindly arm of the law. The dogs are taken to Battersea, checked for health, and then kept for a minimum of seven days in the hope that the owners will call and collect them.

It is a pity that the people who 'lose' their dogs cannot see the creatures' reactions when the ambulance brings them to Battersea after a round of calls. As the van pulls up inside the yard and the doors are thrown open, the smells of a whole new world strike the dogs inside. Bewildered, they sit there without excitement, without the tail-wagging one associates with any new experience for a dog and without the eager inquisitiveness. They make little effort to get out. Occasionally, one of the load will bound forward and lick the attendant, as if he has been lost for a long time and yearns for company, any company. The majority just sit in the van and look a little hurt, yet dignified, as most animals do outside a circus or a zoo.

In an average year about eighteen per cent of the dogs brought in are claimed by their owners; some sixty-five per cent, most of which are sick, are destroyed; sixteen per cent are sold after the seventh day, and immense care is taken to see that these go to good homes and do not end up victims of the vivisection trade or in homes where they will be a nine-day wonder.

The total number of animals dealt with is amazing. In an average year it amounts to about 17,000, mostly collected from police stations; yet the number of dogs reported lost every year is a little in excess of 5,000. The number of stray dogs in the London area has mounted by about 1,000 a year over the last fifteen years. Those who deal with them give a variety of reasons for this. One of the primary reasons would seem to be the movement of people in the London area into flats or different houses. Very frequently a condition of the letting is that 'no animals are allowed' and, whereas a few owners faced with this will take their pet to a home where perhaps another owner can be found for it, the majority just dump or lose them.

There is a growing feeling that far fewer dogs would be adopted light-heartedly as pets, without consideration for the time and trouble involved in keeping and exercising them, if there were a substantial increase in the licence fee. The dog licence was introduced in 1796 to help finance the French wars, and the present figure of 7s 6d (37½p) has been unaltered since 1878. A sum of £2 is levied in Denmark, but an even higher figure would be acceptable to most owners.

The case-history of many of the individual dogs arriving at the Home can be pathetic indeed. There was, for instance, a poodle in fine condition, found with a note written by two children tucked inside his collar. The note explained, in heartbroken terms, that the parents had been on a housing list for a very long time and had at last been offered accommodation – with the rule 'no pets'. So Kim was eventually taken to Battersea Dogs' Home. A few days later, however, a tearful family collected him. They found they missed him so much that they were prepared to forgo the offer of new and better housing conditions. There was a happier ending than most to this episode, for the story appeared in the press and someone was so touched by the family's loyalty that they offered a house where Kim could go too.

Another case involved a Nottingham lorry driver, who called at Battersea in the hope of finding his boon companion, a Labrador, who had jumped from his cab at a busy crossing in London. It was impossible for him to stop at the time and when he could there was no trace of the dog. Some days later, however, the dog duly arrived at the Home. The owner was notified, and picked up his pet on the next trip south.

A crane operator, working on the side of the Thames one day, saw a dog struggling in the water. He made several attempts to rescue it and at last did so, only to find that the poor thing was starving, its ribs jutting through its coat. He took it home and surreptitiously gave the stray the dinner which had been prepared for himself. His wife persuaded him to take the dog to the police station. Not very willingly, he did so, and then got into his car and drove off. When he stopped at the traffic lights farther down the road, he saw the dog he had just left crossing the road in a frantic effort to get to his car. After that there was only one thing for it; formalities completed, the dog was his, and they are today inseparable.

Perhaps one of the most heart-rending cases, while it lasted, was that of the seven-year-old lad who called at Battersea to report the loss of his mongrel. 'You see,' he told the officials with the seriousness of a child, 'he suffers from kidney trouble and he will be very ill without me.' For fourteen days the child called daily and, as his unhappiness was making him ill, his parents too searched high and low for the lost animal. The child's visits to the Home were punctuated with new brainwaves thought up in his desperation. One day he brought a photograph to make sure the officials would recognize the dog when they saw him. The next he reported he had left a light burning in the window all night so that, if his dog saw it, he would know it was his house. Rarely have the staff, who certainly have some pathetic cases to deal with, felt so desperately sorry; but when seven weeks had passed, all but the child had given up hope. Then the miracle happened. A dog answering to the description was brought in. It was the right one, and there was not a dry eye among those who witnessed the reunion between the dog and his young master.

Examples such as these go some way to compensate for the shocking cruelty and neglect which so many of the dogs have met. Some have been wandering for weeks in a starving condition, some are so ill that they can hardly drag themselves along. Among recent cases of bitches turned out by their owners when about to whelp was a small dog who, having given birth to six tiny puppies, stood guard over them so ferociously that even to feed her needed the utmost caution.

Very often the seven-day rule is not strictly adhered to. One man used to bring his dog in whenever the law caught up with him and he received a prison sentence. This was all right until he was given a really long stretch. Even then the Home carried on, and when at last the man was released, his first call was to collect his dog.

One section of the kennels at Battersea is a sad place, for it houses the animals destined to be put down painlessly. Perhaps they have been brought in injured, terribly maltreated or just too sick. There is nothing else for it; they have to die, and anyone looking at them can see that they sense it. Labradors, spaniels, Dobermanns, mongrels, whippets, Alsatians, greyhounds – almost every known breed or intermediate breed of dog arrives at some time or other.

This, of course, is one of the puzzles. One can begin to understand a small mongrel dog not being claimed, but how can one explain a St Bernard or a Great Dane being missing and no one inquiring after it? These large animals are often brought in by the ambulances and obviously do not come from the East End, which perhaps is responsible for the largest number of strays. Fashions in dogs change from time to time and this makes a difference to the activities in the Dogs' Home. Until 1961, for instance, a poodle was a rarity; now the Home is handling between fifty and sixty a year.

The Home traditionally carries three canine residents, and usually they are real characters. One such is Tina. When BOAC was experimenting with a new container for use in jet planes, a request was made for a dog to go on a trial trip and Tina was lent. She flew to Prestwick and back, and acquitted herself very well indeed.

Somewhere in the region of a hundred people a day visit the Home. Some are hoping to find their lost pet, others go to buy one. The way the preconceived ideas of this latter group change before they have been in the place many minutes is remarkable. They arrive feeling quite certain just what they want and spend a long time describing their particular requirements. Then, as they go round, they are unable to withstand the wistful look of one dog, or the pathetic eagerness of another. Generally all their firm resolves melt, and they go off thrilled and triumphant with the last kind of dog they ever expected to possess.

This great Home was founded at Holloway in 1860 by a Mrs Tealby. Her purpose was to give succour and shelter to the waifs and strays of London's dog world and the very idea was greeted with derision and ridicule. Within three years, however, 35,000 dogs annually were being dealt with in a twelve-mile radius of Charing Cross. In 1896, a rabies scare took the number up to 42,000. The Home was removed to its present site in 1871. The work has never been government-subsidized and is financed purely by public subscription. The premises have now been partially rebuilt and thoroughly modernized. The kennels have under-floor heating, infra-red lighting and fibre-glass beds. A staff of thirty-four works under the direction of the secretary, Lieutenant-Commander B. N. Knight, RN (Retired).

In addition to dogs, much is done for cats, nearly 1,000 of these being handled each year. No animal is ever turned away. A fox captured at Canvey Island was given shelter until the RAF unit at Binbrook adopted him as their mascot. From time to time rabbits, and even monkeys, turn up.

There is a large out-patients' department at Battersea, where the pets of old-age pensioners and children are dealt with, some 700 animals paying visits each year.

As a tribute to the foundress, the following verse by Byron appears each year in the annual report of Battersea Dogs' Home:

> *With eye upraised, his master's look to scan,*
> *The joy, the solace, and the aid of man;*
> *The rich man's guardian and the poor man's friend,*
> *The only creature faithful to the end.*

When a Dread Disease Arrived

When a dog in Camberley, Surrey, developed the dread disease of rabies in October 1969, the effects on the local animal world were tragic. The terrier, Fritz, owned by a soldier who had recently completed a tour of duty in Germany, had been in quarantine kennels for the stipulated period of six months. A short while after his release and return home he was seen to be unwell and one morning, foaming at the mouth, he dashed off from the house, bit a milkman and a cat, and returned home. He died shortly afterwards.

Rabies has appalling effects on humans as well as animals, and immediately the Ministry of Agriculture took stringent measures. A warning was sent to 10,000 homes in the area, all dog-owners being faced with the problem of keeping their pets under house arrest for six months. All the strays in the district were destroyed after they had been held by the police for seven days.

It is a sad reflection on the human race that, when the order was made known, veterinary surgeons were inundated with requests to destroy pets; this they refused to do.

A further blow to animal-lovers was the Ministry of Agriculture's decision to destroy all wild life in the Camberley area. There were two schools of thought on this, but those who felt that, although Britain had been free of the disease and its frightening consequences for over forty years, no possible chance must be missed in eliminating even remote sources of infection, prevailed. It was planned that any wild animal big enough to be hit by a shotgun should be exterminated by a team of Ministry of Agriculture hunters, assisted by soldiers.

So one hundred beaters flushed through 3,000 acres of common north of Camberley, and sixty guns waited to bring down anything driven from hiding. Badgers, rabbits, squirrels, foxes, stoats, weasels and anybody's pet cat or dog, if it should wander into the area, were all to die. The day before the shoot, pest officers dropped cyanide powder into fox earths and rabbit holes, to be sealed as the gas filtered through. It was the first time in Britain that such a massacre had been ordered.

Throughout the day police loud-speaker cars toured the common, warning families to keep children and pets indoors in the next two days of shooting. In the event no domestic pets were shot; one greyhound was sighted but he got away. At the end of two days the guns carefully totted up the bag: 13 foxes, 153 squirrels, 2 rabbits, 8 magpies, 12 jays and a crow. The carcases were packed in plastic bags and sent away for examination. None showed any signs of rabies.

The shoot, of course, outraged a great many naturalists and animal-lovers. Many felt it was hard on badgers and that it was ridiculous to think that foxes, voles or squirrels, let alone magpies and owls, could have made any contact with the stricken animal; the chance of infection is limited by the fact that the infected animal's saliva must enter a wound in another animal or human. It was felt that there was an element of panic about the shoot, and that it would have been better if the Ministry of Agriculture had decreed vaccination for all domestic pets instead of the slaughter of wild life.

Then, a week or two later another dog, a Labrador – also from Germany – died from rabies while in quarantine. Fifteen dogs who had been in the same quarantine kennels were placed under house arrest; they were to be muzzled, exercised only on a lead and kept away from humans and other animals for a further six months.

Very soon after these events, the Government made an order extending the quarantine period for animals coming into Britain from six to eight months. Furthermore, a wide range of animals susceptible to rabies are now banned from entry unless destined for zoos or research establishments. Pine martens, mongooses, bush babies, squirrels, civet cats, ocelots, skunks and racoons, among others, are included.

A few weeks after the Camberley affair, a young German visitor arrived at Harwich. She smuggled in with her, a pet dachshund, Danny. The authorities spent a month trying to trace it. The dog was found later by the RSPCA at Blackpool, and the young lady in question was taken to court, where she was fined £50. Her comment: 'I am very sorry, we have no quarantine regulations in Germany!'

In March, 1970, another dog died of rabies nine months after being brought in from Pakistan. The animal had already spent the stipulated six months in quarantine kennels. As a result the government extended the quarantine period for cats and dogs already in the country from eight months to one year, commencing on Thursday March 12th, 1970. At the same time a complete ban on the import of animals into the country was made operative. A committee of inquiry was set up by the government to review the policy and precautions against rabies.

Rescue for a Kitten

Tied to a brick and thrown into the river at Isleworth, Middlesex, Sooty, a five-day-old kitten, was scooped out caked with mud and gasping for life by an RSPCA inspector. But there was a silver lining. The resultant publicity led to more than 200 telephone calls, some from as far away as Wales and Liverpool, offering the kitten a home. The inspector was later awarded the RSPCA bronze medal for the rescue.

Notable Wild Ones

Most Noble of Them All

One of the most noble of all beasts, one that holds pride of place for all who come across it in its wild state, is the red deer, which has roamed parts of Britain at least throughout recorded history. The 'royal' deer of history, it is the largest of British fauna. Exmoor, in the West Country, probably has as many roaming free as anywhere else in England, an estimated 500 to 600. Even so, the visitor who sees twenty-four or more roaming together is indeed lucky. There are, of course, red deer in other parts of the British Isles. A conservative estimate gives the number in Scotland as 155,000. Martindale forest in the Lake District has a few, as has Ireland. In addition, there are small herds in many private parks up and down the country, and small groups which have originated as escapees from parks.

The antlers on a stag are the crowning glory of the species. The first set grows when the animal is twelve months old and each set is discarded annually, a new one growing in place of the old at about the same time of year as the bracken grows on the hillside. The new growth on the horn is covered by a moss-like substance, known as velvet. This serves to protect the horn in the growing stage, when the slightest knock is liable to cause deformity. As the horn matures, so this moss dries up and irritates, and the stag gets rid of it by rubbing its antlers against trees. This moss, is in effect, protecting the blood-vessels of the growing horn, and only when it is removed do the antlers strengthen and eventually become as hard as bone; in the growing stage they are pliable and soft. It has long been a rule of the Exmoor forest that whoever finds antlers may keep them, and it is not unusual for visitors to find a pair where they have been discarded by the stag.

Some of the finest of these animals weigh up to 350 pounds and measure anything up to four feet (more properly twelve hands) to the withers. Like a sheep, a deer has no teeth on the fore part of the upper jaw, but it nevertheless manages to make itself a nuisance to farmers and foresters when it gets down amongst the crops and the young trees in a hard winter. Deer will not eat anything that is not firm and in a field of swedes can cause considerable loss, not so much by what they eat, but by the amount they uproot and discard.

In the mating period (the rutting season) which takes place in the autumn, it can be seen that a stag's antlers are less a weapon than a display mechanism. Rival stags contesting for a group of hinds will lock their antlers and push fiercely against each other, appearing to be in deadly combat; but in reality little damage is usually inflicted, the weaker stag eventually disengaging and galloping off. The hinds produce one calf, usually at the end of May.

Until the 1963 Deer Act was passed, the British Isles was one of the few places in the world where it was legal to shoot a deer at any time and in any fashion, even in the breeding season, if permission was obtained from the farmer owning the land. Only in the West Country was a close season recognized. Now there is a legal close season for all species of deer, though poachers and amateur marksmen still create havoc at times. Deer have been found starved to death, muzzled by snares set by poachers; others have been found with broken legs or jaws caused by men with snares and shotguns, who are said to be getting a high price for venison from city butchers.

In addition to the red deer, there are now five other varieties in Britain, those most often seen being the fallow deer and roe deer. The former can be recognized by their spotted coats and palm-like antlers. There are many in Epping Forest, where they have roamed free since the eleventh century. They are also found in private parks. Fallow deer, like red deer, are destructive, and this led to their extermination on Exmoor in 1851.

The roe deer is a native of Scotland but has been introduced to woods in many parts of England. Its height is about two feet to the shoulder and its weight between forty and sixty pounds. It is very shy and elusive and it lives in family groups rather than herds.

The Londoner, however, need not travel as far as the West Country or the Highlands to find deer, for fortunately they abound in Richmond Park, Bushey Park and Hampton Court. Records show that there were deer in the Richmond area before the land there was first enclosed by Charles I in 1637. They were certainly roaming in the Bushey Park and Hampton Court areas a century before that, and were being hunted by Henry VIII. It is estimated there are now 250 red deer and 350 fallow deer in Richmond Park; in Bushey Park, eighty red deer and 200 fallow deer; in Hampton Court Park, 125 fallow deer.

Motorists are able to drive through these parks, and because of the speed limits, which are stringently upheld, accidents involving the animals are rare. The Ministry of Public Buildings and Works, which controls the parks, is in charge of the deer. In Richmond Park, for instance, they are fed hay and beans, with swede turnips during the winter months. Apart from this, and the work involved during the culling each year, they need no other attention. In Bushey Park and Hampton Court Park the deer provide full-time work for a gamekeeper, plus part-time work for a tractor driver in winter when the deer are fed at least once a day, and twice in particularly bad weather.

Apart from the royal parks, other owners maintain notable herds. There have been fallow deer at Powderham Castle by the River Exe in Devon for nearly 600 years. At present they number about 250; the conditions there seem to be ideal, for so well do they breed that some fifty have to be killed off each year in order to keep the herd manageable. There are also deer at the lovely mansion of Prideaux Place, which overlooks the harbour at Padstow, Cornwall. Four hundred years ago a legend was born that if the deer in the park ever died out, so too would the Prideaux family. At least once the story was almost put to the test, for in 1946 the usually prolific herd dwindled until only six deer remained. Frantic efforts were made to obtain fresh stock, without success, and then when hope was almost given up, the survivors suddenly took on a new lease of life. Thereafter their numbers steadily increased, until today, in spite of repeated cullings, there are about 100 fallow deer running wild in what is probably the oldest deer park in Britain, for it is first recorded in the year 435.

On the island of Arran, Scotland, there are between 1,700 and 1,800 deer and a short while ago a white stag appeared. This very great rarity is running wild in its natural state on the hills but, as is the way with the animal world, by reason of its colour is virtually an outcast, though it does manage to hold a few hinds in the rutting season. The stag has another claim to fame, however: his audacity in raiding gardens, where his favourite meal seems to consist of rosebuds.

The Wild White Cattle

The story of Britain's herd of wild white cattle provides a link with prehistoric times.

The cattle, reputed to be the most ferocious bovine species in the world, have grazed over moorland on the estate of the Earl of Tankerville at Chillingham, near Alnwick in Northumberland, for centuries. They are probably the last survivors of the savage herds which once roamed all over Britain; their origin is obscure, but they are thought to be descendants of the wild ox which inhabited northern Europe in prehistoric times. That species was said to be dark, the bulls being nearly black but with a white dorsal stripe. The Earl of Tankerville advances the theory that possibly the Druids, by a process of segregation and selective slaughter, eventually managed to produce a white animal of the kind they highly prized for sacrificial purposes.

The present herd is unvaryingly true to type and no coloured or even partly coloured calf is ever born into it. The cattle have dark eyes, black muzzles and hoofs, fox-red hair inside the ears and black tips to their horns, when fully developed.

It seems fairly certain that herds of these wild cattle once roamed the Border forests which extended from Chillingham to the Clyde estuary. In the year 1250, a wall was built round the park at Chillingham, and one of the herds was corralled, perhaps for food, perhaps for sport. When the Border reavers made their frequent raids, they were unable to drive away cattle as wild as these, so the herd remained and is still at Chillingham after 700 years. During all this time no extraneous blood has ever been introduced. Certainly the cattle have never been tamed, and today no human can get close to them without very real risk of his life.

A record of 1692 refers to 'my Lord's Beastes' but no number is given. In the last century there were between sixty and eighty. In 1925 there were about forty, but, after the severe winter of 1947 the herd was threatened with extinction, reduced to eight cows and five bulls, all the younger beasts having perished. For eighteen months no calves were born, then a slow process of recovery began until, at the last count, the herd numbered twenty-one females and thirteen males.

Scientists and animal breeders are intrigued by the question of inbreeding, for the mating and breeding is left entirely to nature. The results are carefully watched and the knowledge acquired may one day prove of great value to breeders of domestic cattle. No matter what the size of the herd, the sex proportion has been fairly constantly in the ratio of three females to two males. Nature, by the principle of 'kingship', ensures that only the best blood is passed to the next generation. Only the strongest and fittest bull becomes 'king', for, to obtain the position, he must defeat in combat any bull which challenges him. Inevitably the day comes when he in turn is beaten in battle, and then he is temporarily banished from the herd. He may come back and make another bid for leadership, but, even if he is successful, his new 'reign' will be short. Death in a fight is unusual but it does sometimes occur. From 1947 to 1955 there was only one 'king' bull – quite a long reign. All the present animals are his progeny. They follow ruthlessly the savage law of nature, and a sick or wounded beast, knowing by instinct that it is an outcast, usually goes away from the herd of its own accord; if not, it is speedily ejected by its fellows.

A fascinating fact, that seems to be a throwback to ancient

times, is that the animals have preserved their instinct about natural foes such as wolves. They ignore a shepherd's dog, but if a pack of foxhounds come into the park they immediately form themselves into a close group preparatory to stampeding. If the danger materializes, the hounds coming really close, the herd stampedes in close formation with the cows in front, calves in the centre and the bulls at the rear, the 'king' bull taking up the rearguard station.

There is a resemblance between the Chillingham wild cattle and the shorthorn and the Ayrshire. The bulls weigh about half a ton and the cows some seven hundredweight. Their weight and brawn, however, are deceptive, for in spite of their size one has been known to make a standing jump of six feet.

This amazing breed lives on without the assistance of man. For many years now they have been neither hunted nor shot. They retain their instinctive dislike of the scent of humans but at least they have become accustomed to the sight of man, providing he does not get too close. For man's part, the herd is of the greatest scientific and historical interest.

The cattle are now maintained by a non profit-making body, the Chillingham Wild Cattle Association Ltd. The public may go and see the herd, the park being open on certain days of the week between April 1st and October 1st, and on Bank Holidays. During the winter months the herd may be seen by appointment by parties of not less than four.

Reindeer Graze in Scotland

An interesting experiment, initiated in 1952, has resulted in a fine herd of Scandinavian reindeer roaming today in the Scottish Highlands. These magnificent beasts are an added attraction for visitors to the Cairngorms.

When Mr M. N. P. Utsi noted how the Scottish ground rock and tree lichens, which make up the bulk of reindeer food, resembled those in Lapland, he determined to bring some of his own reindeer over from Swedish Lapland. The Reindeer Council for Great Britain was formed to encourage the scheme, and later the Reindeer Company Ltd, which owns and runs the present herd, was brought into being by Mr Utsi and his wife, Dr E. J. Lindren, an expert on Manchurian reindeer. A first consignment of the animals was permitted to graze on 300 acres inside two miles of six-foot fencing.

The reindeer did well and more were allowed into the country, including some forest types and a few from southern Norway. Then the Scottish Forestry Commission permitted some to graze on a seventy-acre plantation, and immediately noticeable was the lack of fraying of conifers – a welcome change from the ravages of red deer and roe deer who are not so discerning.

In 1954, the reindeer were allowed freedom to graze like hill sheep over the Glenmore National Forest, which comprises 5,000 acres classified as unplantable. The land rises to some 4,000 feet and there the animals have settled down as if in their native surroundings. It was found that, when the reindeer strayed, they usually turned back of their own accord, guided by a strong homing instinct and the attraction of mineral licks. They began to breed, most calves being born in May. The reindeer are evasive but usually quite friendly, except in the October rutting season when a bull may behave in a threatening way. Sarek, an ox from the north of Sweden, led the Scottish herd for twelve years. By the summer of 1969, there was a herd of seventy-one, all born in Scotland.

The great advantage, of course, of keeping reindeer is that they can find their food even under snow, and require no shelter. Reindeer have for centuries been profitably kept in many countries: in Siberia, northern Russia and in most of Scandinavia, while, as caribou, they have long roamed northern Canada. Russia probably still has between two and three million of the species. The introduction of reindeer to Alaska in the 1890s has proved dramatically successful, and there are now about 1,000 in north-west Canada. They are also found in Greenland, South Georgia, the Antarctic, the Kerguelen Islands (French Antarctic) and elsewhere.

The reindeer in Scotland could have many uses; the meat is delicious, and clothing made from the well-tanned hide is worn in temperate as well as in cold climates. Reindeer hair is blended with wool and mohair for expensive dress materials; so far this has had to be imported into Britain. The antlers can be carved in a variety of handicrafts. Research is taking place into reindeer milk, the skin, hair and bones.

Escapees

Every few months yet another unusual animal escapes from private ownership, apart altogether from those which make a break from zoos. Police in Blackpool have had the job of locating a crocodile. A racoon, a possibly dangerous member of the North American family, was caught in Essex, and escaping snakes have given cause for concern in many places.

Air Lift for Budgerigars

Perhaps one of the nicest stories concerns the pet budgerigars belonging to the crew of the Shambles Lightship, which lies eight miles off the Dorset coast. The budgerigars, well-named Ebb and Flow, produced quads.

Soon after they were hatched the youngsters developed sharp appetites, so the Navy stepped in and a helicopter obligingly dropped thirty pounds of bird seed on the lightship.

'Lucky Dog'

The term 'Lucky dog' has become part of the English language, and can usually be assumed not to refer to a dog! There is, however, an eight-year-old cairn terrier who has really hit the jackpot. Sherry had a fortune of £33,000 left to him in the will of his late mistress, Mrs Vera Rae, of New Brighton, Cheshire, who died in 1969, aged sixty-one.

Of course Sherry cannot possibly use all that money, but before any balance over and above his requirements can be passed on to animal charities, some calculation has to be made of how much he will need for his lifetime.

The dog's guardian, Mr John Noakes of Neston, Cheshire, runs a boarding kennels on the lines of an hotel. So Sherry lives in centrally-heated kennels and starts his day with a bowl of milk. He takes his constitutional with a kennel-maid, after which he may have a run round with specially selected friends. For lunch he has a large portion of freshly-cooked meat with brown bread and dog-biscuit. A veterinary surgeon attends him at regular intervals.

Epilogue

Gone are the days when dogs sweated at turning spits or pulling carts: when horses were grossly overworked in cabs and carts. Horses are no longer used, to any extent, in wars, and the day of the pit pony is fast coming to an end.

One would have hoped that this demonstrated a general and ever-increasing improvement in our relationship with animals. On the contrary, most thinking people are concerned at new trends and pause to wonder if man, with his ever-growing scientific knowledge, is not denigrating other forms of life and subjugating them to his own selfishness. Battery farming, which turns poultry into closely confined 'living egg-machines', so that the birds must be de-beaked to overcome the troubles of their restricted existence, is one aspect. Calves are subject to the same imprisonment, and now similar treatment is being tried for lambs. Many hundreds of baby seals are shot each year to protect fishing, but man himself, in spite of his superior brain, is polluting the rivers and by this act alone killing millions of fish.

Only now is some concern being felt about the feeding of antibiotics into livestock to promote their growth. When in 1969 thousands of sea birds were found dead, analysis showed that their bodies contained so many chemicals that it was impossible to determine which particular one was responsible for their death. It would seem that in the senseless and aimless slaughter, man is not only destroying the environment of the animals but ultimately his own as well.

In his book *Vanishing Wild Animals of the World*, R. Fitter states that, in the last two hundred years, at least one mammal every year has become extinct and that there are between 200 and 300 candidates waiting in the wings for the same fate.

The chinchilla, for example, much in demand for its fur, has been practically exterminated in its natural habitat and polar bears are still hunted by so-called sportsmen, who spot and follow them in aircraft, then land on the ice to shoot them.

The worst example of ruthless slaughter known is that of the American bison. Until well into the nineteenth century there were at least 60,000,000 of these animals, which were the main economic asset of the Red Indians. With the advance of the white man into their territories between 1867 and 1871, the slaughter of the bison took place on an unprecedented scale and it was all but exterminated. Only a few isolated groups escaped destruction.

Efforts are now being made to stop the annihilation of many species of animals and birds before it is too late. Great work is being done, but it is the private individual and voluntary organizations which are taking the lead. Governments, as is their way, do too little, and then usually too late. Fortunately, in Britain and the USA many areas are being set aside as reserves, where all forms of wild life will be safe. The lesson is clear. Only public opinion thoroughly aroused can have any effect.

The start of 1970, designated European Conservation Year, saw the most concerted effort yet made on an international scale to encourage people to learn about the environment of animals and to be active in caring for them. Supported by eighteen member countries of the Council of Europe, its aim was to bring to the notice of official and voluntary bodies the need to conserve nature and natural resources.

An example of what can be done if the will and the spirit is there, can be seen at the Esso Petroleum Company at Fawley, Hampshire. This huge oil refinery, built at a cost of £100,000,000 has been surrounded with a green belt of its own, which contains not only a sanctuary for birds but also a wildlife sanctuary. At a time when the wild creatures and even flowers seem to be fighting a losing battle for survival against the sprawl of industrial urban development, this is indeed a break-through.

The problem of encroachment on the countryside is not so much the direct destruction of the wildlife itself, but the often thoughtless destruction of the natural habitat in which it has its being. A detailed survey of the green belt surrounding the Fawley refinery was carried out by the late Major Oliver Kite who, with Mr Ted Channell as camera man, spent twelve months making a film of the wildlife there. No less than eighty-eight separate species of birds, twelve types of butterfly, foxes, voles, moles, squirrels, stoats, rabbits, and scores of other animals and insects were apparently unaffected by the tremendous industrial upheaval nearby and were carrying on their everyday life.

Perhaps most surprising was the wildlife on the mudflats adjoining the jetties, where 21,000,000 tons of crude oil and oil products are loaded and off-loaded every year. Flounders abound, thus providing food for cormorants, and there are large resident populations of waders, curlews, redshanks and oyster catchers. In a fresh-water pond close to the sea, moorhens and mallard breed and heron feed.

This is an accomplished project which holds out great hope for the future. Providing care is taken there is no need for industrial development to sound the death knell for so much that is appealing and beautiful, and which after all has a right to live.

PICCOLO
FICTION
Superb Stories – Popular Authors

FOLLYFOOT   Monica Dickens   20p
Based on the Yorkshire Television Series
FOXY   John Montgomery   20p
FOXY AND THE BADGERS   John Montgomery   20p
THE CHRISTMAS BOOK   Enid Blyton   20p
THE OTTERS' TALE   Gavin Maxwell   25p
The junior Ring of Bright Water
THE STORY OF A RED DEER   J. W. Fortescue   20p
FREEWHEELERS   The Sign of the Beaver
   Alan Fennell   20p

PICCOLO
NON-FICTION
The best in fun – for everyone

CODES AND SECRET WRITING   Herbert Zim   20p
JUNIOR COOK BOOK   Marguerite Patten   25p
BRAIN BOOSTERS   David Webster   20p
PICCOLO QUIZ BOOK   Tom Robinson   20p
FUN AND GAMES OUTDOORS   Jack Cox   20p
FUN-TASTIC   Denys Parsons   20p

PICCOLO
COLOUR BOOKS

Great new titles for boys and girls from eight to twelve.
Fascinating full-colour pictures on every page.
Intriguing, authentic easy-to-read facts.

DINOSAURS
SECRETS OF THE PAST
SCIENCE AND US
INSIDE THE EARTH
EXPLORING OTHER WORLDS
STORMS
SNAKES AND OTHER REPTILES
AIRBORNE ANIMALS

25p each   Fit your pocket - Suit your purse

PICCOLO
FICTION
For younger readers

ALBERT AND HENRY   Alison Jezard   20p
ALBERT IN SCOTLAND   Alison Jezard   20p
